About the Author

Sean Maple was born in April 1936 in Wimbledon, London. At the end of the war his family moved down to Kent. In the 1950s he took jobs which allowed him to continue playing the jazz trombone in the evenings, not giving much thought to the future. Between 1972 and 1975 Sean trained as a teacher. He taught in a county primary junior school until his retirement in 1996. Sean played with various jazz bands until 2019, mainly in East Kent, although he also did weekend tours in Belgium, France, and Germany. Before his death in December 2023, he had published one novel. He was married with three children and three grandchildren.

Hit Man

Sean Maple

Hit Man

Olympia Publishers
London

www.olympiapublishers.com
OLYMPIA PAPERBACK EDITION

Copyright © Sean Maple 2024

The right of Sean Maple to be identified as author of
this work has been asserted in accordance with sections 77 and 78 of
the Copyright, Designs and Patents Act 1988.

All Rights Reserved

No reproduction, copy or transmission of this publication
may be made without written permission.
No paragraph of this publication may be reproduced,
copied or transmitted save with the written permission of the publisher,
or in accordance with the provisions
of the Copyright Act 1956 (as amended).

Any person who commits any unauthorised act in relation to
this publication may be liable to criminal
prosecution and civil claims for damage.

A CIP catalogue record for this title is
available from the British Library.

ISBN: 978-1-80439-451-9

This is a work of fiction.
Names, characters, places and incidents originate from the writer's
imagination. Any resemblance to actual persons, living or dead, is
purely coincidental.

First Published in 2024

Olympia Publishers
Tallis House
2 Tallis Street
London
EC4Y 0AB

Printed in Great Britain

Dedication

I dedicate this book to my daughter, Shelagh Maple.

Acknowledgements

I would like to thank my daughter, Shelagh, for her most helpful suggestions… and my wife, Clotilde, for her help with the computer when I lost parts of what I was writing.

CHAPTER ONE

DUBLIN
Spring 2014

The two men stopped before the cramped little shop, feigning interest in the handwritten postcards pinned inside the display case beside the door; two men waiting by a bus stop. The shop bell sounded – a sudden, strident clang – and a grinning child clutching a newspaper and a pack of twenty cigarettes skated away over the smooth paving slabs. A hand appeared at the glass door and with a deft movement reversed the sign to "Closed". The speeding child turned the corner, and the avenue was quiet again.

'Shouldn't be long now,' murmured the older of the two as they studied the reflection of the estate car parked further down on the other side of the avenue. The image of a milk float, finished with the day's deliveries, jingled rhythmically across their crystalline picture, then shivered to pieces as a bus came to a juddering halt, shaking the ground beneath their feet and rippling the plate glass window. The bus waited just long enough for a woman to alight, then drew away noisily in a cloud of black exhaust fumes.

'Jesus!' spluttered the younger man, putting his hand over his mouth. 'Wouldn't you think they'd fix that stinking old heap? Sure that would give you the lung cancer. Isn't it against the bloody law to go spewing out filth like that?'

'Here she is now,' continued the older man, ignoring his companion's outburst. A tall, blonde woman accompanied by a bounding Alsatian dog walked out of the passage between the Victorian terraced houses and approached the car. Puppy-like, the dog seized the leash in its jaws and pulled at it playfully.

The woman laughed and they could hear her gentle humour in her remonstrations.

'Is that the dog?' asked his companion in incredulous tones. 'Sure it's only an old cod of a dog. Will you look at that? Bloody old softy.'

The dog reared up on its hind legs, stretching its neck to grasp the leash in the woman's outstretched hand. 'It's like an old dancing bear. Should be on Christmas cards,' he continued in disgust.

'You're always ready to take things at face value,' the older man admonished. 'If you were to go near her, that fella would have the head off you. Don't be deceived. It loves her. But it worships him the more. She'll have a hard job now to get him in the car. See.'

Sure enough, the dog, so compliant with the woman's wishes, so eager to please, differed with her over the idea of entering the car. She had raised the tailgate but he just sat, tongue lolling, when she ordered him to jump in. The woman prevailed eventually but only after becoming very firm, and it was a most reluctant dog that slunk finally into the car.

'It's because he's not going too,' the man continued. 'It knows he's staying in the house. When she comes back, it'll shoot out of the car like a rocket and run on in without her... But it'll be all over by then – your man'll be dead and we'll be heading north.' He stiffened, suddenly alert. 'Now then,' he whispered, 'here she goes.'

The car door slammed – a flat sound on the nippy afternoon air – and they watched the reflection glide smoothly across the plate glass as the car accelerated away behind them.

'Not yet,' he muttered crossly. 'Will you wait!'

But his young partner had turned and was moving away, crossing the avenue rapidly. He followed, almost running in his agitation, and caught up as the youngster stepped into the passage from which the woman had emerged.

'Now you just listen to me,' he hissed. 'I say what goes and you do as I say. It's taken us years to find this bastard and there's no way you're going to louse it all up with your feckin' gung ho. Didn't I tell you we were to wait by the shop 'til the car turned out of sight? Did it never occur to you she might be looking in her mirror when you crossed the road? Or that the bloody dog might see you and go bananas?' He emphasized each question by banging the young man's head against the wall. 'I can't believe you did that after all I'd said. You bloody young eejit.' He banged the youngster's head against the wall again to emphasise the last word.

'All right. All right. You're choking me. I'm sorry. I'm sorry. I'm just too tense. I'm so keyed up,' gasped the young man, rebellious but eyes averted, afraid to meet the stony blue of those of his partner. They waited in the cool, dark passageway, each affected by the furious exchange, the older man gritting his teeth, listening for the sound of the returning car, the younger seething with resentment.

'Now,' said the older man at last, 'put on your hood and follow me – quietly and carefully. We've been over this many a time. You know what to do. Are you ready now?'

The young man nodded. They moved cautiously along the cool passage until they emerged from the relative darkness where, conscious of the many overlooking windows, they paused. Here, the rear corners of the two houses met the shoulder-high brick walls which enclosed the alley. Tall wooden gates faced each other, one leading to the garden on their left, the other to the garden on their right. They heard the rattle of lawnmowers being pushed to and fro and, nearby, a woman sang softly, maybe to a child. The alley led on between buff, weathered walls to where it entered the corresponding passage between two houses to exit onto the road which ran behind and parallel with the avenue. At the half-way point was a junction where the alley branched left and right providing rear access to the houses in both roads. They paused, watching two workmen carry a ladder out to the street. The man studied the left-hand gate, noted how well it looked compared with its peeling, blistered comrade opposite. Making sure the two men were gone, he gently eased up the latch and pushed the gate open.

From the garden shed they could hear the brisk clatter of a broom chasing into corners, thumping between bench legs, and driving the dust and shavings out over the threshold with fresh, spring vigour. The older man put a finger to his lips, pointed towards the shed and beckoned his colleague forward. They stole down the garden towards the shed, where he drew the door back slightly to ascertain the situation within. Then, pulling down his hood, he mouthed to his partner, 'Are we good?' and nodded his approval of the lad's thumbs up. The workbench, with their victim kneeling beneath, stood to the right-hand side.

The man inside, on his knees now and sweeping beneath the bench with a hand brush, whistled a breathy accompaniment to his exertions – partly out of good humour and partly to blow the rising dust away from his sweating face. Suddenly his whistling turned into a gasp of surprise as the dark spiders fled in panic before his searching brush.

'God Almighty. Did you ever see the like?' he muttered in amusement. 'Fiona!' he exclaimed, as he felt the floor flex gently under the approaching footfall. 'Mind how you come in here. There's big fellas down here well able to run up your leg.'

He laughed as he began to back out from under the bench. 'All right, me hairy lads. Panic's over. Aren't I cleaning the place for you? Won't you be all spick and span now 'til next time?' But his banter died abruptly as he saw the shining oxblood shoes, and the fear he had confined to a distant corner of his mind for all those years suddenly surged – acid in his throat. Despite the many precautions that had been put in place, they had found him. Desperately, he thrust his body backwards to clear the confines of the bench, to rise to his feet, to grapple with the intruder, to fight for his life, or... But the assassins had every advantage.

The older man dropped to one knee and, as his gun boomed the first round into the back of his victim's head, the door was wrenched open and the snarling dog was on him, closely followed by the raging woman. He threw up his free hand, grasping at the thick mane as the charging animal's momentum forced him onto his back. His gun struck the metal vice behind him and discharged at the same instant that his partner shot the dog. His partner took the stray shot through the chest and slumped to the floor.

Impeded by the inert body of the dog, the gunman was unable to parry the woman's ferocious attack. She drove her long fingernails at his eyes. He roared in agony and anger, 'Bloody bitch,' and ramming the muzzle of the gun into her neck, squeezed the trigger.

The gun misfired. It misfired again and a crawling fear took hold of him as he recognized the overwhelming madness in the woman. Her fist pounded into his face and scrabbling fingers clawed at his eyes. Again and again, she drove her knee at his groin, but he had managed to find some protection by inching himself backwards until the dog's hindquarters slid down between his legs.

He thrust his left hand under her chin, forcing her head back and back again, squeezing her throat, but she fought on, frightening him with her ferocious strength; punching and clawing, her breath rasping as he failed to crush her windpipe. Her hands were inside his hood now, her nails scoring his face like hot blades. Twisting her head suddenly and evading his grip, she bit down hard on the gloved hand. She realized that the first finger of the glove was empty at the very instant that the gun crashed into the side of her face. She tasted blood and heard his breathless voice as if from far away. 'Bitch. Bloody English whore,' as the heavy gun struck again and again…

He pushed the heavy bodies away and, rising to his knees, listened. The ragged heave of his own breath was the only sound as he crouched there in that shambles, conscious of the incongruity of the woman's perfume mingling with odours of cordite and dog and the dusty atmosphere.

'Someone's pissed their drawers,' he muttered as the stench of urine was added to the thickening brew. Reaching across her blood-soaked hair, he felt for his partner's carotid artery. There was no sign of life. Squatting there, he leant back against the bench for support then, having regained some degree of composure, stood up and dropped the bloodied gun into his deep coat pocket.

Standing there, dabbing at his bleeding face, he studied the dog. Why had she come back? Had she seen them crossing the road and become suspicious? The wide chain collar was missing from the dog's neck. Had she simply come back for that bloody collar? He hadn't noticed it was missing when they got into the car. As a rule, it was not the sort of detail he would miss. It had gone against the grain, having to keep the lad in order – watch his every move in case he fouled up. That wasn't the way he liked to do things. It had not occurred to him until now, but the boy's edginess, his thoughtless, headlong approach to the operation could well have been down to a drug habit. He'd been so confident, so eager, but so careless. And now he was dead. He looked down at the body dispassionately.

'You were on something all right, boyo,' he muttered. 'God, you must have thought you were bulletproof, you bloody young hophead. Ah well, it's over now all right.' He sighed, stooping to retrieve the young man's weapon.

He felt a sudden stab of anxiety as the full significance of his own situation began to dawn. He'd done his best, used every bit of influence available to him to resist the order that he was to work with the young partner. And now this. He had a serious problem. If the garda found the bullet that had killed his partner, their ballistics records would show that the gun had been used in several other killings too. Of itself this wasn't a serious problem all the time he kept the gun safe, but what did matter was that his own people would soon gain possession of the information and, unlike the garda, they would know that the gun was his. They would surmise that he had pulled the trigger. He had objected to the arrangement in the strongest terms, but it had all been in vain. He had suggested some good men – men with proven records of dependability – men whose professionalism matched his own, but new faces were giving the orders these days and he'd been forced to acknowledge that he no longer commanded his former degree of respect.

'They're going to say it was me that shot him,' he murmured. 'No one's going to believe it was an accident. Why would they, given the way I've acted?'

He had become a fugitive. He would have to drop out of sight, disappear before he found himself on the receiving end of rough justice. He felt some relief because he'd made plans – an escape route and a false identity. But he was going to have to move quickly.

'Well,' he mused, 'I'm George McDermott from today. Thank God that's all in place.'

He looked at the dead man beneath the bench. 'There's a good few who will be glad to hear that you're a goner, Frankie bloody Jackson, you bastard turncoat spy. God Almighty, what a bloody mess.'

Looking at the row of bright chisels above the bench, he shuddered as he dabbed at his bleeding face with his blood-stained handkerchief. He checked through the open door then ran lightly down the passage. Cautiously he peered round the front corner of the house and looked out onto the avenue. As the saloon car drew out and approached, there was no one else to be seen in either direction. He jumped in, slamming the door and settling back on the leather seat.

'Drive!' he ordered. Left and left again.

'Got it,' said the young driver, as the powerful car surged away from the kerb. 'Job done?' the young driver asked, meeting his gaze in the rear-view mirror.

'Job done,' replied the gunman, taking off the bloody hood and stuffing it into his pocket.

'What happened your face? You look as though you've been in some fight all right.'

'Things didn't go to plan back there, turned into a fiasco,' he replied wearily.

'They told me there'd be two of you.'

'Whisht now. Eyes on the road, eh.'

The driver glanced up at his mirror into the cold blue eyes of the gunman and saw that he'd said all he was going to say.

He made no comment as they passed the estate car parked at the end of the alley, its tailgate open and the turn signal pulsing regularly in the afternoon sun.

The bodies lay undisturbed through the long warm afternoon and into the early evening and might have lain so for days, but for the banging of the shed door.

CHAPTER TWO

Old Eddie Bonner stirred in his sleep. He laid there puzzled by the streaks of sunset shining through the threadbare curtains, invading the darkening room and reaching across the ceiling. Something odd, something out of place had roused him from his afternoon stupor. He was drinking heavily these days and had long since given up climbing the stairs to his bed, having taken instead to sleeping on the old settle in the parlour. He tried to ease the crick in his neck and let out a troubled sigh as he attempted to massage away the stiffness. Raising himself onto an elbow, he groaned and as he reached for his cigarettes and matches, he heard the bang of the shed door.

'Oh boys oh boys,' he muttered, as the sulphurous fumes induced a fit of wheezy coughing which, for all its hacking violence, failed to delay the lighting of the fag. The flaring match accentuated the shadowy corners of the room, while the tobacco calmed him as he took a deep drag and drew the smooth smoke deep into his lungs. He leant back, his head wreathed in spirals of hanging, blue smoke, and thought about making a move. Then, as he tottered experimentally to his feet, the shed door banged again.

'Honest to God,' he exclaimed. 'How would a bloody saint put up with the likes of you for neighbours? Bad cess to you. Nothing but banging and bloody dog barking the whole of the day. And if it's not that, it's the bloody sawing and drilling all hours like a bloody factory.'

Old age and too much solitude had turned Eddie into an intolerant man. Very little pleased him these days. He pulled on his old jacket and made for the back door, grumbling the whole time, his baleful remarks punctuated by the slamming of the shed door.

He tottered out from the back kitchen and along the path to his back gate. It was secured of course, and he found it difficult to draw the rusted bolt. This bruising exercise increased the foulness of his temper so that, when he finally managed to force open the swollen gate, he was in no mood to ask them to secure their bloody door; he would damn well do it himself and if they objected, well he was ready for that too. He had plenty to say to them all right. He thrust their gate aside and strode down the garden towards the shed. He pushed the door to close it, but he felt it twist against an obstruction at the bottom.

'God damn it to hell!' he blazed as he slammed it repeatedly to no avail. It was too dark to see what was impeding the door so he knelt to feel if he could move it. 'Mother of God?' he gasped, as his hand closed round the clammy, coldness of the woman's ankle. He recoiled in fright, wiping his sticky hand on his trousers.

He stood for a moment, irresolute in the gathering darkness, shocked, and then, making the sign of the cross, he reached in to find the light switch.

'Would you listen to old Eddie out there?' Unlike Eddie's dilapidated home this room was brightly lit, a picture of comfortable domesticity. She looked at her husband, expecting a response to her remark.

'Ah, leave him be,' he said, settling back into his armchair. 'He's just feeling good. He likes a song, doesn't he? If we just ignore him, he'll soon quieten down. In a minute he'll go into

Don't cry for me Barcelona. You know the way he is.'

'It's Argentina.'

'What is?'

'In the song. It's Argentina. You said Barcelona.'

'I'm only saying what it is he sings. He's so drunk half the time he doesn't know what he's singing.'

She sighed as she resumed her ironing. 'It's well poor Bridie can't see the state of him now or hear his drunken roaring.' She was about to add that it wasn't good enough to just go on ignoring Eddie, that he needed help, that they were supposed to be his neighbours, but she simply sighed, knowing from experience that it was better left unsaid. Eddie had repeatedly rejected offers of help, to the point that her husband had completely lost patience with him. Poor Bridie had been her best friend since they were schoolgirls together. But the cancer had taken her, and Eddie – God help him – had never got over it.

The sudden banging on the front door brought her to her feet with a startled gasp. 'John. Who could it be?'

Her husband, equally alarmed, rose to his feet but, before either of them had moved, the parlour door flew back and Eddie Bonner stood there looking even more dishevelled than usual. His lined old face wore the expression of a man in shock.

'Ah, God help me,' he sobbed, moving forward, hands spread in supplication. 'God help me. Will you come quick? It's next door. Oh God. Oh God.' He shook his head from side to side, a man in despair.

She uttered comforting words, moved to him quickly and supported him towards a chair.

'No!' he cried. 'It's no good. Come quick. I put on the light and I seen a vision of Hell in there.' He paused to bless himself. 'It's Con lying there in the shed with the face shot off him and poor Fiona too lying dead and the old dog whining and snarling if you go near. There's a young lad and I think he's shot too. What'll we do? We have to do something.' Eddie staggered and almost fell in his agitation.

As she clutched at his arm to save him, her husband said, 'Stay here, Marcia. Mind him. I'm going to find out what's happened round there.'

'No!' she cried, but he was gone and she had poor Eddie to cope with.

CHAPTER THREE

'Get a bloody vet' here now,' shouted the garda inspector. 'That damn dog is holding everything up. I was told he'd be here half an hour ago. This is a murder enquiry. Goddammit, it's a double murder enquiry. Maybe more, for all I know. Our people have to get in there. I want that dog dealt with. Will you move your bloody arse?'

The harassed young garda picked his way through the muddle of arc lights, cables, media crews and garda personnel, made his way out to a garda car and spoke into the handset.

The scene was one of confused activity. Under the stark glare of the arc lamps the garda tried to bring some order to the night. But they were unable to approach the shed where the bodies lay, because the big dog stood guarding the door. Despite its wound, it had dragged itself to the threshold. Dark blood caked its coat, glistening under the white light. It was obviously in distress, but it waited, head down; defiant. Different garda officers had tried to approach but, having witnessed the animal's explosive fury, there was not a man there prepared to try again.

There was sudden activity in the alley and two young men made their way towards the impatient police inspector.

'Trouble with a dog?' asked the first.

'I should say so,' snapped the inspector, suspecting levity and pointing to where the dog stood guarding the shed door. 'You took your bloody time. Now whatever you're going to do, do it now, quick as you like. We've been held up too long already. Shoot the bastard. We've a job to do here.'

'He's just doing his job, you know,' smiled the vet. 'He surely is a grand dog. We'll anaesthetize him and remove him as quickly as possible.'

'You'll not get near that bastard. I've never seen anything like it. That bloody dog would eat you alive.'

The vet smiled. 'We have ways, you know. I've no wish to get bitten myself.'

The second young man reappeared, carrying a lightweight rifle, and together the two of them selected a dart, cocked the weapon and moved to a better vantage point. The dog, ever watchful, snarled and dropped into a crouching attitude. The vet raised the rifle and took careful aim as his assistant moved slowly towards the dog. The dog growled and gave a warning bark. The man moved closer and as the enraged dog turned its body and began barking furiously at him, the vet squeezed the trigger. The dog yelped as the dart smacked into its shoulder. It stood head down with legs spread wide for an age before sliding gently to the floor and half rolling over.

'Very neat,' cried the inspector in admiration. 'Well done, lads.'

'I need to move him quickly now,' said the vet. 'He's lost a lot of blood. I hope we haven't overdone it. The sooner we get him into surgery, the better. We have a stretcher ready. Would some of your lads give us a hand out with him? He's going to be a real heavyweight.'

'God Almighty!' cried the young man, as he leant over the dog. 'There are dead people in here. Did you know?' He stood pale-faced, pointing to the interior of the shed.

'We do,' answered the inspector, taking his arm and leading him away. 'If you're going to puke, mind my shoes. That's why we've been so anxious to get in there. So now if you and your boss move the bloody dog away, we can get on with our job at last.' He beckoned to the garda. 'Give a hand here, lad. Help them carry Fido out.'

'Doesn't care for dogs, your governor,' said the vet, as they manhandled their heavy burden through the gate and into the alley.

'No, he doesn't,' replied the garda. 'When he was a lad, his father's dog attacked him one day and he was badly bitten. They do say it bit his arse so I guess he was running away.'

'Nasty. An experience like that would stay with you forever. What happened to the dog?'

'I don't know. Evidently, it had never bitten anyone before. It's my guess he tormented it. I think it should have been given a bone. He's a terrible man, very difficult to work with being so short-tempered. Good luck now. I hope the dog's going to be OK. Well, I'll go back now and see if I can do something right before the end of my shift.'

He waved them off and trudged back along the alley.

And so, with the dog removed, they were at last able to approach the shed. The inspector stopped at the threshold and studied the carnage within. After observing the bodies of the woman and the young man, he adopted a crouching posture to view the third body beneath the bench.

'Jesus,' he muttered, as his torchlight came to rest on the ruined face.

He stood back to allow the medical team to enter. The first of them stepped in, taking care, as far as was possible, not to disturb the scene as he checked for signs of life. The inspector turned to the young garda. 'It's an execution,' he said. 'Your man was killed with one to the back of the head it looks like. But the other two? I don't know.'

As he started to reach for his cigarettes, he heard the excited voice from inside. 'I've a pulse here.' The medic stepped out into the cold glare of the floodlights. 'The woman's alive anyway. We have to get her to the hospital as quick as we can.'

'The young fella?' asked the inspector.

The medic shook his head. 'No. The other two are stone cold. Been dead a good few hours, I'd say.'

'Will I pass on your opinion to the good pathologist?'

'Only if you want to get on his wrong side. He'd be real peeved if he thought bloody paramedics were horning in with their opinions.'

'I'll try to keep him sweet then, the ould bugger,' said the inspector as he gave them a broad wink.

In a very short time, the limp body of the woman was lifted with expert care and stretchered out to the waiting ambulance, leaving the garda personnel to begin the investigations. They worked the scene throughout the night and would be there well into the following day, searching, collecting and photographing, compiling such meagre evidence as came to light – the beginnings of their enquiries, which would be long and quite probably fruitless. As always happens in such cases, there would be the usual news reports on the killing, and neighbours would voice their outrage about a murder being committed in their road, and what a dreadful thing it was to happen to such a popular couple. Marcia would smarten up old Eddie, even to putting one of her husband's ties on him, for his TV appearance as finder of the bodies, a performance he would relive many times for his audience down at the local bar.

Then would come the inevitable leaks to the media and furious denials all round before the whole affair was overlaid by the next big story and soon forgotten.

CHAPTER FOUR

As the investigating officers worked on through the night, across the city the woman lay pale and still in the hospital bed. The ward was in darkness except for the subdued glow from the electronic equipment monitoring her vital functions, and the small lamp where the sister on duty worked silently at her desk. The soft sounds emanating from the equipment impinged on her consciousness as gentle, friendly voices; she would know immediately should there be a change in the woman's condition. Nevertheless, she rose from time to time, approached the bed silently on her rubber soled shoes, studied the equipment and the various tubes and bags, and recorded her findings on the patient's chart.

Everything that could be done had been done. From the moment she had been placed in the ambulance, the woman had received the best of medical care. Whether she would survive the night remained to be seen. Severe trauma followed by hours of lying unattended in the shed had brought her to this low ebb. The spark of life was faint and in the dark hours yet to come it might just diminish and fade away despite the best efforts of the medical team.

'Your poor face,' murmured the sister as she leaned to look closer at the woman's battered features. She stood listening to the soft bleep of the oscilloscope and watched the undulating, green line travel across the screen, recording the beating of the woman's heart – encouraged and somewhat reassured by the regularity of it all.

Elsewhere in the awakening city, the young vet was watching the dog. It lay on its side, breathing regularly. As in the case of the woman, everything that could be done had been done and, as with her, the dog's survival now depended on its constitution.

The assistant came in with two mugs of coffee and chocolate biscuits.

'It's getting light,' he said, passing over one of the mugs then placing the biscuits between them.

'Thanks,' said his colleague.

They sat in silence for some minutes. Long hours spent at the practice had inured them to the cocktail of animal odours, disinfectant and blood, so they munched and drank contentedly, relieved to have finished the task and done all that could be done for the wounded dog.

'Isn't he a grand old lad?' said the vet at last. 'I think he'll be all right. You'd never imagine the bullet would've taken that path. In by the sternum, around the outside of the ribcage and out the back of his neck. Bloody amazing – a pretty clean wound really and no great harm done apart from the heavy blood loss. Let's hope the antibiotics handle any infection. The analgesics will keep his pain in check.'

'You'll want me to stay while he comes round?' asked the assistant.

'I surely do. Can't have him thrashing about when he wakes up – 'twould undo all our good work.'

'You do have the muzzle handy?'

'I do,' the vet replied with a grin. 'I've no wish to be savaged by my own patient.'

'Then I'm your man.'

The two young men continued their vigil in silence.

The assistant yawned and stretched, rose to switch off the lights then returned to slump into his chair.

'I'll brew us some fresh coffee,' said the vet, getting to his feet and stretching his arms wide.

'Call me if he stirs. Oops, sorry, no pun intended. Put it down to lack of sleep. Aah! Sorry again. I don't seem to be able to stop. My tongue has disconnected from my brain. I'll say no more.'

He carried the cups through to the kitchenette as the young assistant blinked his tired eyes and tried not to think about the grisly sight of those bodies lying in the shed. He watched the rhythmic rise and fall of the dog's chest.

'Well, you're a fine old fellow in repose,' he murmured. 'Let's hope you're in a good mood when he wakes you.'

CHAPTER FIVE

Oliver Flynn moved quickly to drop out of sight, to emerge again as George McDermott. Everything he needed to achieve this was to hand in the safe under his bedroom floor, and his contingency plan was soon set in motion. In the days when he was first deciding on his escape strategy, the big question had been where to run.

England was always favourite, simply because he was familiar with much of the country, having lived and worked there as a sleeper in an IRA cell. Prior to that, he had served a term in the British Army, taking part in the first Gulf War, Operation Desert Shield.

As a member of a Special Services Unit, he had taken part in several covert operations but was flown home for specialist surgery when his left hand was badly mangled by shrapnel from an Iraqi shell. It looked at first as if he would lose the hand, but thanks to his surgeon's dedication and skill it was saved largely intact, missing only the index finger.

After many sessions with a very demanding physiotherapist who refused to take no for an answer, he regained about 60% of normal movement, flexion and a reasonably strong grip and, while it would never be as good as it was before, it was infinitely better than having to use a prosthesis. The physio told him that more improvement was quite possible if he continued with his exercises. However, it meant that his service days were over. There he was, a young man, skilled in close combat and the use of small arms, a perfect recruit for the IRA.

He proved his worth on several IRA operations, both with his marksmanship and his ability to think on his feet when the unforeseen cropped up. The Provisionals' Ceasefire in '94 and the Good Friday Agreement in '98 brought peace to Northern Ireland but, as evidenced by the Omagh bombing in the August of that year, not every faction was happy with this. Much of the bitterness would never be forgotten, and shootings would occur from time to time as old scores were settled, the demise of Conor O'Brian, real name Francis Jackson, being the most recent of these.

The downside of choosing England was that those hunting him would know his old haunts. Even so, he felt better able to avoid detection when on familiar ground – better able to hide in plain sight as it were.

He had limited knowledge about English-speaking countries beyond the United Kingdom and felt that as a recent arrival to America, Canada, Australia or New Zealand, he would attract attention. There were Irish communities to be sure, but there were also regulations, visas, permits and the like – all designed to keep tabs on aliens. The idea that he might be classed as an alien did not appeal to him at all.

In the end, it was a no-brainer. He'd known what documentation was required and how to get hold of it, genuine or otherwise, and the English way of life suited him very well.

So, he had assembled all that was necessary under the alias George McDermot, together with a quantity of ready cash – all of which he could access quickly. His ace in the hole was the small-bore pistol constructed of non-metallic components, worn in an ankle holster. He only had a dozen rounds of ammunition, but he planned to collect a weapon with more stopping power once he arrived in England. He had two extra counterfeit British passports of very high quality, each bearing his photo, each in a different name, and two corresponding bank accounts were in place. Tinted glasses, a peaked cap, maybe a beard and a change of hair colour, together with extreme vigilance, would have to suffice in the short term. Eventually he might arrange to have his appearance altered surgically.

All of this had cost him a great deal of money, money amassed through robberies, smuggling and other nefarious activities but now, on finding himself in a position so similar to that of his most recent victim, aka Conor O'Brian, all his careful preparations were fully justified. His own situation was even more perilous than O'Brian's because both the garda and the RUC would be after him, as well as the IRA.

Of course, he was under no illusions about the single-minded tenacity of his pursuers. He knew exactly how thoroughly they would set about tracking him. Hadn't he just been on the team that found Conor O'Brian? And O'Brian had the advantages of help from the British Government – witness protection, change of identity and all the rest of it. But his mistake had been his decision to relocate in Ireland, albeit Eire and, having seen the outcome of this choice, George knew he had to go further afield.

His time as a terrorist and assassin seemed over. Through no fault of his own he had become the fugitive.

CHAPTER SIX

George McDermot boarded the ferry at Dun Laoghaire and made his way to the bar. Even with all his precautions in place, passing through Customs and Immigration had been a worrisome ordeal and he felt much in need of a drink. The bar would remain closed until the ship sailed, and a queue of fellow drinkers soon began to form behind him. *At least I'm first in line*, he thought as he studied the other passengers covertly.

No one stood out at first, but then a large, balding man with an expensive SLR camera hanging from its sling strode in and proclaimed, 'Oh I say. Not open yet?' to nobody in particular and stood smiling. He then raised his camera and took a photograph of the saloon area before continuing, 'Damn shame, I'm as dry as a stick.' Again, he smiled.

This arrival shook McDermot. He became even more anxious. *Who is this guy?* he wondered. *Why would he take a photo? Jesus, he could email my photo to anybody.* He continued to watch closely as the man stood waiting and smiling. McDermot knew he had to get hold of that camera and was considering ways of achieving this when the bar shutters clattered open and the tall red-headed barman demanded, 'Who's first then?'

The balding man, who had moved himself up the queue without provoking any protests from the others, turned his smile on McDermot and gestured for him to go ahead.

'You're before me, old chap,' he said, smile still in place.

George nodded in acknowledgement and ordered a pint of Guinness with a whiskey chaser.

'How about yourself?' he asked. 'Have a drink with me?'

'Well, I must say that's frightfully kind of you, old boy. I'll have a pint of bitter if it's all the same to you.' They took their drinks and moved away to a table.

'Well cheers,' said the large man, taking a long swallow. 'Ah, I was ready for that. Splendid.' He smiled, smacking his lips in appreciation.

McDermott was puzzled by this man who seemed to be smiling most of the time yet wouldn't quite meet his eye. *He's a caricature*, he thought, *ex-public school. Upper class English? Poseur/conman? Or is he an IRA man keeping me under observation? Puts me in mind of Bertie Wooster*, he mused. *He's hamming up the English gent a bit though, a 1930s throwback? No one talks like that anymore, do they?* He realized that the man was offering his hand.

'Alan Goldman,' he said as they shook. 'Jolly nice to meet you.'

'George McDermott,' replied George, momentarily flustered at being caught daydreaming. Alan rapped his glass on the table.

'Same again, George?'

'Sure, but just the porter this time.'

'Ha ha. You Irish chaps and your porter. Jolly good. Won't be long.'

George watched as he made his way to the bar, somewhat unsteadily as the ferry was by this time meeting the open sea. He was just making up his mind to follow Alan and fetch his own drink – much safer to have a hand free when the floor was heaving under your feet – when Alan turned and took another photo.

'What's with all the photos?' he asked, as they made their wobbly way back to their seats.

'Just my hobby, old boy,' replied Alan. 'I paint a bit and I collect images I might find useful. I hope you don't mind?'

'Why would I mind?'

'Well, I've got a couple of good ones of you. You're very photogenic, you know. Quite the brooding Celt.'

'I've never been called that before,' said George with a grin.

'Artist's eye, old boy. Artist's eye. I'd like to snap a few more if it's all the same to you.'

'Sure thing,' said George, deciding he was going to get hold of that camera one way or another. He thought maybe a trip to the gents might present the best opportunity. If Alan meant to send the photos, he would probably head for the loos so as not to be seen – least of all by George.

'Sorry?' he said as he became aware that Alan was talking. 'I didn't catch that, miles away.'

'I asked you if you came on board as a foot passenger or by car?' Alan repeated.

'Oh, I'm on shanks' pony, Alan. I'll hire myself a motor when we get in.'

'Maybe I can drop you off, save you the trouble. What do you say, old boy? Save a few shekels as well? Where're you going?'

'Wimbledon. I've a friend there. I said I'd drop in,' replied George, delighted at this unexpected development.

'Oh yes? Pretty, is she?'

'It's not a woman, Alan,' said George, somewhat testily.

Alan put a hand to his mouth in mock alarm. 'A man. Oh, my goodness, let's not go there, eh?'

On realising that his attempt at banter had fallen flat –

certainly George failed to recognize it as such – Alan adopted a more serious approach.

'I'm going to my studio in Kentish Town. I could drop you off at your nearest tube. It's no trouble, really.'

'Alan, that's a very kind offer. I'm delighted to accept. You'll save me a bundle. Let's have another.'

'Soft drink for me this time, George. Got to think of the old licence, what?'

CHAPTER SEVEN

'That sounds to me like a serious pastime, Alan – the painting I mean – if you've a studio and all. It sounds real professional to me.' They were back at their table sipping drinks.

'I couldn't claim to be a professional, George. I do manage to pull off a few sales when we mount an exhibition, but I'd never make my living at it.

'It's just a hobby really. Oddly enough, it's portraiture that brings the most success. I avoided it for years because I just couldn't do it, couldn't create a satisfactory likeness but, as with a lot of life's problems, if you keep having a go then things often come together. I think people like a portrait that shows the essence of the sitter – a hint of mood, disposition – a facial expression that chimes with their memories – particularly when it's a departed loved one – rather than a photographic reproduction. In fact, I've come to find facial expressions quite compelling, more important by far than photographic representation. But then what do I know? Just a self-taught dabbler, that's me.

'I've no end of still lifes and various landscapes stacked against the wall and, though I say it myself, some of them are rather good, but no one wants to buy them. So, I concentrate more on the old physiognomy these days, hence the photos of you. However, thus far most commissions that come my way are for pet portraits and those clients do want a photographic likeness. I have to say though that when I get it right, it's very satisfying. I feel quite proud of myself when the owner is pleased with my work. I completed one quite recently – big bright-eyed Alsatian dog. The owner was delighted – said Bruce was smiling at her. I got a great deal of satisfaction both from the results of my labour and her reaction to it, not to mention the nice fee.'

'Well, if you happen to like dogs, I suppose. I wouldn't trust a bloody dog as far as I could throw it – treacherous buggers in my book, turn on you in a flash – especially the big bastards.'

For the first time in their conversation, Alan looked put out. 'I can only suppose you've been unfortunate in your contact with dogs then,' he said in a cool voice. 'And I dare say that if we could go into it, irresponsible ownership would be at the root of the matter – properly raised and disciplined with kindness, a dog makes a wonderful, loyal companion. I've a pair of Alsatians and they are completely trustworthy in all situations.'

'OK, Alan. I didn't mean to upset you. Can we not agree to differ? You like them. I don't. It's not something to fall out over, is it?'

'No of course not, old chap. Not if we're going to rub along all the way to London. No more dog talk then.' The smile was back in place.

'Fine by me,' answered George, with a smile of his own.

CHAPTER EIGHT

Disembarkation at Holyhead turned out to be so easy. George was braced for a repetition of his ordeal at Dún Laoghaire, so he was surprised and relieved when the tired-looking immigration officer took a cursory glance at their passports and waved them through. Customs and Excise personnel stood impassively behind their counter, pale-faced under the bright lights.

'Must be the lateness of the hour,' said Alan in a theatrical whisper. 'What a disinterested looking bunch they are, must be on a work to rule or some such. Good job we're not up to mischief, eh?' Alan laughed as the big Audi surged forward.

'Do you make this trip often?' asked George, settling into the luxurious leather seat.

'Couple of times a year, I suppose. I've got relations in Wexford and Kilkenny, and since I've retired I've got a bit more time for them. I love Ireland, often think I'll move there permanently – bit fed up with London, truth be told.

'Sure, there's a lot to be said for the old country,' said George. 'I know both of those places well and I can just picture you in an old cottage – you and your dogs walking the lanes. Which way are we going?'

'A55, A5 to Shrewsbury then M54, M6, M1 all the way to the metropolis. We'll pull in for a bite to eat quite soon. I know a couple of all night places that do good food.'

'Sounds good to me. Tell you the truth, I'm not a very good sailor so I never really fancy anything on the boat, but I'm feeling a few pangs now.'

'Good man.'

'Do you have family, Alan?'

''Fraid not, old boy. All grown up and flown the nest. Two boys – well, young men now. Then when they'd gone, wife took off with a policeman. Floored me at first, hard to accept, you know. Made a bloody mess of it all really. I thought we were OK, you know. But there we are. What's done is done. Just me and the dogs these days, but I don't dwell on all that – what's the point? Keep busy, that's the answer. If it can't be changed, then bugger it. Just have to soldier on eh, old chap?'

'I'm sorry, Alan,' said George simply. 'I didn't mean to pry.'

'Not at all, old chap – not a secret – no harm done. What about you?'

'Oh, free agent, me, Alan. No family ties – never really felt the need to settle down. Couldn't afford it in my younger days. Then when I could, I'd got used to being on my own. It's better that way, I was never a team player anyway. I'm just fine as I am.'

'I'm sure you are, George; know what you want from life, eh?'

George leaned back into the comfort of the leather seat and contemplated the double row of overhead lamps stretching ahead into the darkness; an aerial display predicting every distant curve and undulation of the motorway.

'We'll stop in a minute or two for some supper,' said Alan. 'Actually, I'm bursting to do a pee. We get off at the next exit.'

'Me too,' said George, 'and you must let me pay for the meal. It's only right – you doing me such a big favour and all.'

'That's fine by me, old chap; thank you very much; most kind.'

Alan reduced speed then turned off into a restaurant car park. George reached down to check his pistol, watchful now, fearful in case this was a rendezvous arranged by his erstwhile colleagues. Perhaps gunmen were waiting. It was their way, after all.

Alan swung the car round, reversed expertly into a marked bay and switched off the ignition. There were a few cars parked close to the building where two bright lanterns illuminated the area, but the furthest end of the car park lay in shadow. George peered in vain, trying to see if men were waiting there between the trees.

'Quite a mild night,' said Alan. 'Leave the coats in the car, I think.'

As Alan turned from locking the car, George pivoted suddenly, delivered a powerful punch to Alan's throat and was on him as he began to fall. Putting one arm round his victim's neck, he reached round with his free hand and wrenched Alan's chin sharply to one side, breaking his neck instantly. It was over in seconds.

Shielded by the car, George crouched, watchful, listening. Still he waited, pistol at the ready. All remained quite still, save for the sound of the occasional passing car. He started nervously — from nearby came the sharp cry of a vixen, an accusation borne on the night air – then shivered involuntarily, wrinkling his nose in disgust as he caught the strong smell of urine running from Alan's relaxed bladder.

Placing his weapon within easy reach and pulling on a pair of gloves, he began to go through the dead man's pockets. Mobile phone – a much more up-to-date, sophisticated model than George's own – various credit cards, all in the name of Alan Goldman, a wad of cash, a photo of two smiling boys, a diary which seemed innocuous enough at first glance, several receipts and scraps of paper, together with two monogrammed handkerchiefs and a bunch of keys. He extracted the cash — pounds and euros – transferred it to his own wallet, removed the expensive watch from the lifeless wrist, and dropped everything into Alan's tote bag, having first removed the SD card from the camera and pocketed it along with the car keys.

What to do next? George decided to place Alan's body in the boot and drive the car back to Holyhead so that when it was discovered, there would be nothing to indicate which way he'd gone. *Just the end of a trail gone cold*, he thought as he manhandled the heavy corpse into the boot. He went to the darker end of the car park, stepped in among the trees and did a much-needed piss – all the time watching the restaurant for signs of life. No one arrived. No one left. *Nobody'll ever know we were here*, he thought as he zipped up. He grabbed at a branch as he almost fell into a drainage ditch about six feet deep running through the copse, and immediately saw a new solution to what to do with the body. *It could lie there for months*, he thought, *far enough from the restaurant and it doesn't look as though many folk come up to this end of the car park. Maybe it's busier in the summer and someone will get a whiff of it then. So what? I'll be long gone.*

George reversed the car up to the far end of the car park and lifted the heavy body once more, then rolled it into the bottom of the ditch. Hanging onto a convenient branch, he kicked as much of the leaf mould and dry leaves as he could down on top of the late Alan Goldman until he was satisfied the body was hidden from view.

'That should do it for a time,' he murmured, checking the restaurant for signs of activity and still seeing none. ''Course if they have a bloody dog, it'll soon come to light. Can't be helped, time to go anyway.'

The drive back to Holyhead was uneventful. George parked in a side street and fell to fitful dozing and sleeping, untroubled by any pangs of conscience, only stirring when the sounds of the burgeoning new day chivvied him into wakefulness.

Once fully alert, and having gathered his thoughts, he decided to leave the car where it was then, after wiping down those areas where he might have left fingerprints, took out his suitcase and the tote bag, locked the car and went in search of an all-night café. He was ravenous.

Feeling much restored after scrambled eggs, toast and a mug of strong tea, George selected his second passport, hired a car for a week and with his new identity, Kevin Byrne, headed for London.

'No more George McDermott,' he mused aloud as he drove south. 'Whatever happened to him? Bought a ferry ticket to England and disappeared off the face of the earth. Well, he's gone now all right.'

No more Alan Goldman either; a most pleasant, somewhat naïve man – well-liked for his mild eccentricities. He had been most unfortunate in attracting the groundless suspicions of a paranoid killer when he'd taken those photographs.

CHAPTER NINE

'Your man is gone, I tell you. The guys have looked everywhere and there's no sign of him. He's away.' The fat, sandy-haired man spread his arms wide to underline the message, then leant back, elbows resting on the bar.

The two brothers seated in the snug bar sat contemplating him, their faces set in grim expressions. 'You're quite sure?' asked the elder brother quietly. 'Have you tried his place again?'

'All locked up and no trace of him.'

'You went in?'

'It's locked up, I tell you. So no, we didn't go in.'

'Well, get your useless arses back there and get yourselves inside! Jesus, must I do everything myself?' he roared. 'Get in and search it thoroughly – you'll maybe find a clue or two – I will have that bastard – don't you dare come back here empty-handed.' He stood and slammed his glass on the table to emphasise his anger, then sank back into his seat as the fat man made a hasty exit.

'Brian,' he called. 'You're getting sloppy, I think. Mend your ways. You don't want to piss me off.'

Brian left the pub, walked slowly to the waiting car and subsided into the front passenger seat.

'That didn't go well at all, Tom,' he said to the driver. 'We're to go back and turn Ollie's place over and we'd better come up with something or there'll be bloody hell to pay. God, he went mad in there. You wouldn't want to be Ollie Flynn when they catch up with him. Come on, we'd better get on with it.'

He sat back with a heavy sigh as the car eased out into the Belfast traffic.

Inside the pub, the younger man looked hard at his brother.

'Joe. I'd like to hear Oliver's side of it, you know.'

'Oh you would, would you? How's that then? Do you not believe in evidence? We both know Flynn couldn't stand Eugene, said he couldn't work with him, said he wouldn't work with him. I had to get very heavy over it. Eugene was shot with Flynn's bloody gun and we know they didn't get on.'

'If you hadn't forced the issue, our nephew would still be alive and we wouldn't have to see his mammy in such deep distress. Our own sister and she can't look at us.'

'Are you saying it's all my bloody fault, then?' Joe rose to his feet red with anger, glaring furiously at his younger brother.

'Joe. I'm simply saying I'd like to hear Oliver's side of it.'

'Well, we'll just have to see if I can get him to tell it to you before I put a bullet in his brain. Why do you think he's gone on the run? Are you completely feckin' stupid?'

'Maybe he's innocent but thinks we'll never believe him because of all the fuss he made over being forced to take Eugene as his partner. I mean, just look at his record, Mr. Reliable, never a blemish – a perfect soldier, great in a crisis, a real professional. Why would he shoot Eugene?'

'We don't know the why. We only know it was Flynn's gun and he's fled rather than face us.'

'Circumstantial, Joe,' said his brother. 'And we both know Eugene had his problems.'

'That's enough, Liam. You're questioning my judgement. You're out of order. I won't hear another feckin' word.' Joe's lips were flecked with spittle as he raged at his brother. 'Maybe the lad wasn't perfect, but he didn't deserve to be shot down like a dog. Stop now, right there. The subject is closed.'

'I'm not saying you're wrong, Joe, just that there's more to this than meets the eye. It's not like Oliver, that's all.'

Joe slammed the door on his way out, leaving his brother looking defeated and concerned that as a senior commander Joe was so entrenched in his views. *Is he losing it?* he wondered. He'd sensed the fear underlying his brother's bluster. As a teenager Liam had seen his father's mental disintegration as he'd slipped away into his separate world of dementia and he was finding Joe's recent behaviour extremely disturbing. *Is it his turn now?* he wondered, and as the implication sank in, not for the first time, *is that in store for me as well?*

He's about the same age me da' was when his troubles started, he mused as he placed the empty glasses on the bar and shrugged into his coat to go home.

CHAPTER TEN

Kevin paused in his writing and looked fondly round at his small, comfortable saloon. It pleased him no end to gaze at the furniture and fittings in his unusual new home. The idea had come to him quite suddenly one bright morning as he was strolling along the Regent's Canal towards Camden Market.

He was enjoying the holiday-like atmosphere, mingling with the good-natured crowd and, despite his concern to remain vigilant, felt himself being drawn into it all. The combination of beautiful weather and relaxed people with a smile together with the colourful, gently chugging boats was a seductive mix.

Pausing to lean on a bollard, he singled out a particular boat as it approached, observing details he'd never really noticed before; ropes neatly coiled, ready for use, wonderfully decorative pails and planters on the roof, gleaming brass fittings and the name painted on the side panel, "*Greta*". Everything so spick and span.

A suntanned woman in her forties, wearing cut-off jeans and a yellow sleeveless top, sat reading a paperback on the foredeck and, as if sensing his interest, she looked up and smiled. Kevin put up a hand and smiled back as she glided by. He wondered if her name was Greta. Then came the tall, bearded figure at the tiller and Kevin was struck by his relaxed posture and expression. He wore a baseball cap and a light green singlet which showed his tanned arms and shoulders and as he reached to adjust the throttle he smiled up at Kevin and shouted, 'Great morning, eh?'

'It surely is,' answered Kevin. 'You're looking good on it, anyway.'

'Isn't everyone?' replied the man, gesturing at the people all around.

'Guess they are,' said Kevin, nodding and smiling. The man waved, then called, 'Greta.'

The woman appeared, pushed the fenders over the side with her foot and stood holding the coil of rope, ready to step off as the helmsman slowed and angled the boat in towards the bank.

Kevin, continuing his walk, was deeply impressed by the couple on the boat. He dwelt on the man's rapt expression as he'd stood at the tiller. *That was pure contentment*, he thought, wondering at how he was so deeply affected after such a brief encounter. *It's envy*, he thought. *I'm jealous.*

Maybe that's it, he mused as the thought struck him quite out of the blue, – a *narrow-boat? A floating bachelor pad. Why not?* He would be on the move, albeit at walking pace, but who would expect him to take to the water?

He gave a lot of thought to the idea and visited the library, where he discovered a rich source of information on canals of the British Isles. It soon became clear that one could cruise for weeks on end on the extensive network of canals in Britain.

He read back numbers of *Waterways World* and found much to encourage him in the many articles and advertisements. After all his reading and talking with boat owners, he had learned a lot about the maintenance and berthing of narrow boats. He still had some reservations, for example, could he live on a boat through the winter? So to allay his fears and find out just how he would fare as a "boater", he hired a neat two-berther described as half a narrowboat and, after a few tips and a short trial run with the owner, he was on his way. One moment the man was instructing him on the best way to moor up – the next, he was saying, 'Off you go then, skipper. Have a nice trip,' as he turned to walk back to the boatyard, leaving Kevin dumbfounded at the abrupt nature of his departure.

So brief was this course of instruction that Kevin proceeded with extreme caution at first and was most grateful for the help and advice from the crew of the boat ahead of him when he arrived at his first lock. After a day of cruising and negotiating further locks, however, he had the feel of the boat and was enjoying the experience immensely. *Everyone is so friendly*, he thought, *and helpful too, like joining a club where the members all make you welcome.*

This new world quite fascinated Kevin. He found himself thinking about ancestors who'd quit Ireland in the eighteenth century and crossed to England, looking for a better life. *I wonder if any of them became navvies*, he thought. Did they send money home to their families? Or did they work hard and spend hard on drink; forget all about the folks at home? What a massive undertaking, to build such a vast system of canals with the technology of those times; what vision. All done with pick and shovel, wheelbarrows and human sweat. Then there were all those brilliant engineers and surveyors, men with expertise, able to design, plan, and have such confidence in their levelling work, to know that when the water was let in, it would lay in the channel exactly as they expected.

Then look at the locks. What a marvellous idea, would have to be a clever guy to come up with that. *I guess there must have been a balls-up or two to start with.* He smiled. Just imagine it. Fill her up, lads. And then, when you come back in the morning, Where's all the bloody water gone?

It was while cooking breakfast on his third morning that he'd realized just how much he wanted to continue this life on a boat of his own.

'I'll call her *The Happy Wanderer*,' he'd murmured as he'd thrown left over bacon rinds and toast to the ever-hungry ducks and swans.

He'd found his boat for sale in a boatyard on the Thames. It had been specially built to a high specification for a middle-aged, overweight businessman who, on doctor's orders, had decided it was time to lead a healthier life-style. Like so many before him, he was over enthusiastic, went at it like a bull at a gate and suffered a cardiac arrest on his second week afloat. The family wanted a quick sale and so Kevin was able to buy himself an excellent, two berth, beautifully appointed boat, complete with fully equipped kitchen, towels and bedding, even to the tasteful set of impressionist prints hung in saloon and bedroom, at a knockdown price. He had the name, *"Let's Go!"* removed and she became *"The Happy Wanderer"*.

Now here he was, moored for the night, a beer at his elbow, recording the events of the day in his log. As well as the pleasure he took in maintaining his boat and cruising at his leisure, he had developed a keen interest in the flora and fauna of the canals. He turned to books again, read avidly and was soon able to identify many of the birds and small mammals he came across each day. Hour after hour, he stood at the tiller, rain or shine, binoculars to hand and felt a huge thrill every time he recorded a new sighting or managed to photograph a moorhen or coot shepherding youngsters across the water. He sometimes wished that he'd hung on to Alan Goldman's camera but the tote bag and its contents were weighed down with bricks at the bottom of the Thames. Anyway, his little compact produced excellent photos and was simple enough to operate.

Pretty well everything about life on the canals suited him perfectly. Managing his boat, locking, finding a mooring and so on required forethought, particularly for a solo boater. Ropes had to be arranged so that he could manage locking and mooring from the stern and he was quick to appreciate the potential for disaster if he approached these events at too high a speed. He had become proficient in a short time and being in sole control was what suited him best. His beard, after an uncomfortably itchy start, had grown quite quickly and though it had too much grey in it for his liking, he felt it suited him, as well as helping to alter his appearance.

He enjoyed drinking in the many excellent canal-side pubs and met so many interesting people but then became uneasy about the possibility of being spotted. Because of his accent, fellow drinkers would often ask where he stood regarding a united Ireland, which made him feel uncomfortable. The more belligerent drinkers tried to draw him into discussions about the IRA attacks on the British mainland and became quite heated, in their efforts to provoke an argument.

I can't be talking about stuff like that, he thought. *Draws too much attention*, and so his visits became fewer and fewer until he almost stopped altogether. He always felt vulnerable walking back along the towpath in the dark. 'Too bloody risky,' he told himself.

Loneliness had never been a real problem for Kevin. He enjoyed female company as much as the next man but, apart from a couple of flirtatious encounters, one of which involved an attractive but rather predatory landlady, he steered clear for safety's sake. He missed his evening visits to the pubs and restaurants at first, but soon became accustomed to spending his evenings on board, with the television for company when the signal was good. He updated his journal regularly and he had plenty of reading material including a daily paper, usually the *Daily Telegraph*. Recently, he'd read of the discovery of Alan Goldman's body. He was pleased to read that the police had only the one lead: Mr Goldman had been seen on the ferry in the company of an Irish man known as George McDermott; they had issued a description and were appealing for sightings of him with the usual warning not to approach him as he might be armed and dangerous.

'You'll be lucky,' he'd murmured with a smile. 'That description could be almost anyone and old Georgie is long gone.' He was relieved to see there was no mention of his missing finger.

He altered his routine to having a pub meal most lunchtimes, less risky in daylight, and making do with a snack on board in the evenings.

At the back of his mind, he knew that his idyll could not go on indefinitely. He still had plenty of money, but it wouldn't last forever and his pursuers would not rest until they found him – but he refused to dwell on his problems. He would have to make up his mind about what to do when winter came – carry on cruising or book a temporary mooring and decide whether or not to renew his licences and insurance.

'Of course, I'll stand out like a sore thumb when all the holiday boats are laid up,' he mused. 'Should I sell the boat and just take off? *Que sera*,' he would murmur whenever thoughts about the future crossed his mind. He remained ever vigilant, unable to reach a decision but determined to enjoy each day as it came.

'This'll do me,' he mused, gazing raptly round at the interior once again.

He pulled out a drawer, reached in and lifted out the revolver; hefted it and spun the cylinder several times. 'No misfires with this baby,' he said. 'Uncomplicated, like me.'

CHAPTER ELEVEN

Fiona's recovery was slow at first but once the bruising and swelling of her face had largely disappeared, her rate of recovery became quite remarkable. The hospital staff were delighted with her progress and just that morning her consultant had congratulated her.

'You know when they brought you in, you were in a pretty bad way, Fiona, but look at you now. I've seen a good number of horrific injuries in my time and the resilience and powers of recovery of the human body still amaze me. You'll be discharged soon and then when the dental work is all finished, you'll be good as new. Everyone is so pleased for you. What plans have you for when we let you go?'

'I can't thank you all enough,' said Fiona. 'It's all been such an ordeal and I'm so grateful for the way you've seen me through it all; the pain and discomfort – the depression and everything – everyone's been so kind.'

Her voice began to break and she paused to blow her nose and waited a moment to regain her composure.

'To answer your question, I've decided to sell up and go home to England. My parents want me back home and now Conor's dead I've no reason to stay. They have a lovely cottage near Bray – that's near Windsor – and my room is all ready for me. They want me to bring Bruno too, which is just marvellous. I couldn't bear the thought of leaving him behind. I'm so excited. I've such a lot to look forward to, finding a job for example. I must have a fresh start and going home is the first step. I have so many happy memories of being with Conor, but he lied to me. All this stuff that's come out about him working for the British Army, infiltrating the IRA, informing and so on and the media calling him a hero; it's all been such a shock. He put me in danger – I didn't even know his real name. I feel... betrayed by it all. Staying on, especially in that house, is out of the question.'

'Maybe he felt you were safer not knowing,' said the consultant.

'I've wondered about that too, but I just wish he'd been honest with me from the beginning. You know that day began like any other – routine – shower, breakfast, read the paper, prepare lunch... walk the dog... just another day in the lives of Conor and Fiona... then it was all gone in a moment.

'I drove off with Bruno in the back as usual, but he became agitated quite suddenly – one moment he was sitting up looking out as usual, then he went berserk, whining and throwing himself about with such violence that I had to pull up to see to him. I thought it was a fit. Then when I raised the tailgate he came out like a bullet, knocked me aside and dived into the alley. That's when I had this awful premonition, I knew then as I chased frantically after the dog that Conor was in trouble.

'I heard the first shot, then another, as I wrenched open the door. Poor Conor lay under the bench and Bruno, lying dead, as I thought, on top of a hooded man with a gun. There was a second man down on the floor further inside. I froze for a moment trying to take in the awful scene before me. The gun – the hooded man – the gunfire still ringing in my ears and then I felt an overwhelming surge of hate and went for the gunman. I wanted to claw him to pieces... Well, as you know, I got the worst of that and the murderous bastard is still out there.

'I still have awful flashbacks and nightmares where I'm running endlessly along the alley, desperate to get there before the gunshots and always failing. Sometimes, it's more than I can bear. I'm just hoping that this will all go away when I've moved back home.'

'It's going to take time, Fiona, but I think you're wise to move away. Perhaps as you engage with your new life these unpleasant after-effects will begin to fade and leave you. I strongly recommend that you continue with the counselling, at first anyway.'

'Just remember we're all rooting for you,' he continued, smiling and placing a hand on her shoulder. 'You deserve to be happy. Good luck and don't forget us, all toiling away in old Ireland.'

'I'll always remember my time spent here,' she replied. 'You've all been so wonderful.'

The first thing Fiona did on being discharged from hospital was to order a taxi and go straight to the veterinary practice where Bruno was being cared for. She shed tears of joy as the huge dog bounded up to her and did his best to knock her off her feet. His joyous barking and exuberant leaping up to lick her face was quite out of control for a few minutes, but with help from the vet and his assistant she managed to weather it all. At last Bruno calmed down sufficiently for Fiona to express her gratitude to the two young men for looking after him so well, but when it came to settle the bill she was surprised at how reasonable it was.

'This can't be right,' she said, pointing at the total. 'On top of all his treatment you've boarded him for weeks.'

'Ms. Murray,' replied the vet, 'the bill is for treatment only. This old chap is such good company I couldn't possibly charge you for his keep. We've been dreading today because we would love him to stay. Life won't be the same round here when he's gone.' He smiled ruefully as Bruno moved to sit next to Fiona, looking up expectantly.

'This fellow knows what we're talking about,' he went on, 'and he's ready to leave.'

He reached down and scratched the dog's head, but Bruno's shining eyes remained fixed on Fiona. 'See what I mean?' he laughed.

Despite Fiona's protests he refused to move on the bill, but had no objection to her making generous donations to the animal charity collection tins on the counter. At last she was ready to leave. She shook hands with the young men and once more expressed her gratitude for their devotion to Bruno's wellbeing.

'Oh, before I go, I'm taking Bruno with me when I go home to England and I just want to be clear about his passport, Conor always dealt with dog stuff. May I bring it in for you to check?'

'As long as he's microchipped and his rabies vaccination is current, you'll be OK, but bring it in by all means and we'll have a look. If he does need the anti-rabies vaccine, it must be administered at least twenty-one days before you travel, so make sure you leave yourself plenty of time.'

'Thank you. I can't say how much I appreciate everything you've done for him,' she said, tearing up once more.

'Go on now, ma'am, it's been our pleasure,' said the vet, holding the door open.

He watched the pair walk away and turned to his assistant. 'Well, that was some reunion, eh?'

'It surely was. As soon as she came through that door, we were yesterday's men.'

'Well, that's how dogs are,' replied his colleague. 'Like kids. They don't do tact, just loyalty, plain and simple.'

CHAPTER TWELVE

Kevin's peaceful afternoon was shattered quite suddenly by the ringtone of the mobile phone in the drawer. He paused, cup half-way to his lips. The shock was instant and powerful, like a sudden punch to the solar plexus. Only one person knew the number of that phone, so it could only be bad news.

He slid open the drawer, pushing the revolver to one side and lifted the phone to his ear.

'I'm here, Kenny.'

'They know you're in England,' a man's voice; shaky.

'Go on.'

'I had a visit, two of them. Not what you'd call friendly.'

'How long since?'

'This morning. They know you're here. They know you have a gun.'

'How will I know them?'

'About our age; the talker, average height, overweight, blue eyes, florid complexion, sandy hair, eyelashes, eyebrows, hair receding, double chin, pink piggy features and a real nasty way with him, a bully. The quiet one is shorter, stocky build, dark with plenty of five o'clock shadow. Both wearing dark suits.'

'What else have you told them?'

'That's all. No, tell a lie, they asked me where you were exactly and I said I didn't know but that you had said you were thinking of going to America.'

'That's it?'

'Yes. I'm sorry.'

'No need. You did the right thing. If you hadn't told them, they'd have kicked it out of you.'

'They had a razor. They threatened my family. I didn't want them involved.'

'They're not. You've told them what they want. They won't be back.'

'How can you know that?'

'I know – just trust me. Thanks for the heads up. Now get rid of that phone.' Kevin broke the connection, removed the SIM card and battery from his phone, went up on deck and dropped it all into the canal.

He felt no sympathy for the predicament in which Kenny found himself – he'd been very well paid for his services and understood that with money like that there might well be comeback. He'd entered into their transaction with eyes wide open, prepared to accept the risk.

'So,' he said, 'Brian Fitzgerald and your bloody sidekick, Tom Kelly, coming after me.' His mind went back to his early days in the IRA when he was teamed with Fitzgerald and Kelly to chastise a young woman who was involved with a British soldier. Along with a good many of his colleagues, Fitzgerald did not like Oliver Flynn and made no secret of the fact. They were suspicious of him because of his British Army service and he suspected the beating was to be a test of his commitment.

They'd sat in the pub watching her having a laugh with her friends on what looked like a girls' night out and when she went to the ladies' toilet, they made their move. Kelly stayed at the door to stop any interruptions while Fitzgerald and Oliver followed her in. He would always remember the dismay on her face as she turned to see who was behind her and realized what was about to happen.

He could still see her swollen features as Fitzgerald gave vent to his hatred and beat her unmercifully – her blubbering pleas as she begged him to stop – the blood, tears and snot dripping from her nose and chin, her blonde hair hacked with the razor lying in bloody clumps on the floor. The smell as she vomited. He had stood by while Fitzgerald thrashed and humiliated the defenceless girl. He'd wanted to drive his fists into Fitzgerald's bloated face, but he'd done nothing because Fitzgerald was watching him closely and he knew any betrayal of his feelings would be reported to their commander.

At last, managing to keep his voice steady, he asked, 'Are we to kill her then?'

Fitzgerald stared in surprise, still in the grip of his violent rage, then released the girl suddenly so that she fell to the floor in a sobbing heap.

'No!' he shouted. 'We are not.'

He yanked his victim to her feet and bellowed into her face, 'You're a disgusting whore of the English. What are you?'

He repeated this several times, crushing her breast in his huge meaty hand until she whimpered, 'I'm a disgusting whore of the English.'

'You betray your countrymen when you shag British soldiers,' he grated, looking into her battered face. 'And I'm going to send him home in a body bag. Will I give him your love first?'

She collapsed at his feet crying, 'No. No. Please God no. I won't see him again.'

'You won't, you little slut. I'll make sure of that.'

They'd left the wretched girl sobbing on the floor. He'd burned with shame at the contemptuous stares of her friends as they rushed in to help her.

'And now he's here looking for me,' Kevin muttered.

The man on the phone was an old buddy from Kevin's army days, one of those characters who seemed able to lay hands on just about anything, no questions asked. Kevin had asked him to get the revolver, being under the impression that here was a contact unknown to his pursuers. *Well, I got that one wrong*, he thought as he reviewed his situation. However, it had been a stroke of luck to plant the notion of going to America in Kenny's mind. Kenny couldn't say anything about the canal boat because he'd known nothing of Kevin's plans. In fact, Kevin hadn't even thought about a boat himself at that stage.

'They've no reason to make the connection,' he mused as he lit the gas under the kettle to make a fresh brew. 'I'd have to be real unlucky for them to find me. With a bit of good fortune they might even follow up on the America story.'

Feeling that the odds were still very much in his favour, Kevin prepared to continue his journey to reach Berkhamsted that evening. Before setting off, he went below, took the revolver from the drawer and checked it over. Then, dropping the weapon into the front pocket of his smock, he started the diesel engine, retrieved his mooring stakes and set off.

Standing at the tiller, on the move again, he thought how difficult it would be to trace him, given the vast extent of the waterways in Britain. 'And they don't even know I'm on a boat at all,' he murmured, feeling reassured by his reasoning and by the weight of the gun in his pocket.

CHAPTER THIRTEEN

Joe was smiling as he dropped the phone into its cradle. It was good news.

Brian and Tom, following his suggestion, had been looking up old contacts of Oliver Flynn's over in England. They'd drawn blanks at first as none of them had seen or heard of him for years. However, they sensed that these were serious enquiries; they were all fully aware of the two Irishmen's line of business and extremely keen that no suspicion should fall on themselves, so they were very helpful. But it all seemed to be leading nowhere until they came across a man who had served in the same unit as Oliver and he suggested that they talk to someone called Kenny, another old soldier. This seemed more promising and, after a couple of false starts, they found said Kenny eventually, drinking in a south London pub.

He began by denying knowledge of anyone called Oliver but came clean as soon as his visitors made themselves very clear about ways they had of extracting information and made explicit threats against him and his family. Thus, Brian was able to ring old Joe and inform him that Oliver Flynn was after all in England.

'That's grand work, lads,' said Joe. 'Is this Kenny straight up?'

'He is. He nearly wet himself when I put the razor on the table. He sold Oliver a revolver and ammo, so we know he's armed.'

'That won't save the bastard. Well done, lads – now keep

looking and keep me up to date. We'll fly over when you have him located.'

Liam came into the bar. 'Who was on the phone?'

'Brian Fitzgerald. They've traced an old friend of Oliver's from his army days and he's seen the bastard and set him up with a gun.'

'So, what do we know exactly?'

'More than we did before. He's definitely in England. Evidently, he told this Kenny fellow that he might go to America, but I think that's bullshit – meant to throw us off the scent. We'll have him now all right. It's just a matter of time.'

'Could be, but we know he's a slippery bugger.'

'He can't run forever, Liam. We always find them in the end,' Joe said grimly. 'Just like the Mounties, eh – always get their man. Let's drink to it,' he smiled, their recent altercation clearly forgotten.

CHAPTER FOURTEEN

Fiona's return to the family home was rather strained at first. As she stepped in through the front door, she couldn't help but remember her acrimonious departure when she had flung out of the house vowing never to set foot there again. Her parents had thoroughly disapproved of Conor and had made their feelings very clear at the time but now, after his murder and the anxious hours spent at her hospital bedside, they were only too pleased to have her home again. There was not the slightest hint of 'We told you so' and she reproached herself for having expected that there might have been. Her loving parents' unconditional welcome brought a lump to her throat and she cried in the privacy of her room – cried for Conor, for what might have been, for herself.

Bruno's introduction to the two family springer spaniels, Jack and Jill, went without incident. After much exploratory sniffing and wagging of tails, they settled down amicably and the family would come to enjoy many long walks in the company of their inquisitive trio of dogs.

On the Grand Union Canal, Kevin stood at the tiller enjoying the warmth of the afternoon sun on his back as he continued south. He felt tired but happy after a pleasant but busy day. *I suppose I'm beginning to feel my age*, he thought. Just that morning, he'd studied his face in the mirror and, deciding he was beginning to look like Robinson Crusoe, he took the kitchen scissors and gave his beard a careful trim. 'That's better,' He smiled. 'That's taken years off me.'

Approaching Berkhamsted, he noticed the odd behaviour of

a heron standing at the edge of the water. Each time the boat drew level, it flapped into the air and flew ahead to wait and then repeat the process. He'd observed this performance on previous occasions, but was still unable to account for it. *Maybe he's watching to see if the passage of the boat will throw up a tasty snack*, he thought. Could it be the same bird each time? Now there's a notion that fellow could fly miles while I'm chugging along, locking and the like. He picked up his binoculars and looked in vain for a distinguishing mark.

'Just another heron,' he muttered, 'all look the same; don't even know if it's Mr or Mrs. Is that your party piece?' he asked the heron, 'or are you all at it?' The bird simply flapped into the air, flew ahead and took up a new position.

It was while studying the bird's intriguing behaviour he thought he caught a whiff of burning. Unable to see any obvious reason for this, he moored quickly, tying just the centre rope to a convenient bough, and went below to check. *Nothing wrong here*, he thought, after a good look around. Pausing to clip the fire extinguisher back into its bracket, he went up to continue his journey, feeling rather relieved. The heron had given up on him and gone elsewhere in search of something tasty.

There it was again; just the faintest smell of smoke. *Must be someone with a barbecue*, he thought. *The Canal Trust people sometimes burn rubbish – it could be them.* He continued, happy in the summer sun, soothed by the steady rhythm of the diesel engine rumbling tirelessly beneath his feet.

He slowed as he approached the lock, noting the number 56 on the gate.

Locking is a straightforward affair, usually made easier by the helping hands of fellow boaters, but today he was all alone and would have to manage this one on his own, the lock being empty with the lower gates left open. After mooring the boat, he contemplated the task ahead. *Ah, may as well get on with it*, he thought. Closing the gates and winding down the paddles then going back up and raising the upper paddles to fill the lock left him feeling rather breathless; he was glad to sit and let the sunshine warm his overtaxed muscles while the lock filled. The sound of rushing water was pleasantly relaxing too and he felt a pang of regret when it stopped, telling him the lock was full. Getting to his feet, Kevin opened the lock gates and using his front rope, drew the *Happy Wanderer* into the lock, secured her, closed the gates behind and lowered the paddles, enjoying the clinking of the ratchet and pawl mechanism. 'Canal music,' he smiled. Then he went to the lower gates and raised the lower paddles to drain the chamber, allowing his ropes to run through the rings as the boat descended slowly to the lower level. He grabbed a beer from the fridge and sat down to drink, feeling quite weary.

He'd come through fifteen locks or so since leaving Marston Junction, but this was his first single hander of the day. Unusually, traffic on the canal had thinned out and he felt daunted by the fact that there were over thirty locks between him and Uxbridge.

'That's what I call intensive,' he murmured, looking at his Pearson's Guide. 'Ah well, I can rest here tonight,' he mused. 'I'm sure to meet more boats on the way down tomorrow. But if not, I'll moor up if it gets too strenuous. No point in killing myself. I'm in no hurry and I have to admit I'm not so young anymore.'

He opened the lock gates, gathered his mooring ropes and prepared to exit. As the *Happy Wanderer* nosed out of lock 56, the smell of smoke was suddenly stronger and as he entered the winding hole Kevin saw the burning boat to his left: a small, fibreglass cruiser, bows into the bank, thick, black smoke issuing from the interior. *That's plastic foam that's afire*, he thought. *Hope no one's inside. It's bloody toxic.*

A stout woman stood waist-deep in the water, shrieking, gesticulating and pointing. Turning to look, he saw the pale face of a boy floundering in the water. Turning the boat, preparing to haul him inboard, Kevin steered toward the struggling boy, relieved to see he was wearing a buoyancy aid. Reaching out to grasp the boy's collar, he was astonished to see the infant in his arms. His right hand clutched the material firmly and he lifted the pair from the water, placed them gently on the deck and looked back at the scene.

Two men had entered the water and were trying to assist the frantic woman toward the bank. She was still waving her arms and shrieking and one of the men was shouting and pointing back toward the lock, but the words were all but drowned out by the rumbling diesel under his feet. Turning his attention to the children, he was relieved to see both of them staring up at him with wide eyes.

'You OK?' he said to the boy, who remained tight-lipped but nodded vigorously. 'Is this your little sister?' More nodding. 'You're a brave lad,' he said. 'You did well to keep her face out of the water. You should feel proud of yourself.' The boy screwed up his eyes but remained silent.

Kevin reached down to where the boy sat holding his sister and patted his shoulder. The only reaction from the lad was a trembling of his lips.

'Cry if you want to, son, there's no shame in it. Sure I can feel a tear coming on myself. It's only the reaction.'

'They're in shock,' he said to himself. The last thing he wanted was to become involved with the people from the burning boat so, much to the consternation of the woman and of his two young passengers, he surged away with all speed. There was by this time a group of bystanders gathering at the burning boat.

'Don't worry now,' he said to reassure the boy. 'I'll put you down on the towpath just here under the bridge and you can run back to your mammy. It'll be safer than trying to moor up near all that panic. They've got enough on their hands as it is.'

The boy remained silent and it was obvious that both children were cold and in distress. The little girl began to whimper and her brother held her tight, stroked her wet hair and talked quietly to her.

'That's a good lad. See if you can cheer her up,' said Kevin, smiling. The boy just stared, his pinched features neither friendly nor hostile as the baby's grizzling grew louder.

Kevin stopped the boat under a bridge just long enough to lift the pair onto the towpath. 'There we are,' he said, pointing the way. 'Now go back along there to your mammy and warm yourselves.'

The boy stood shivering, holding on tightly to the baby, water dribbling from their wet clothes, both staring wide-eyed as the *Happy Wanderer* drifted slowly away from them.

'You're a sensible lad, now tell your folks to be careful if there's a gas bottle in their boat. It could explode in the heat of the fire.'

'Thanks, mister!' the boy shouted at last. The baby began to cry in earnest and Kevin saw the two men running towards the children.

'Go on!' he shouted, pointing. 'Back to your mam.'

'Well, he didn't have much to say for himself,' he murmured, as he watched the boy turn away, clutching his wailing burden.

'Shock,' he said, shaking his head. 'Poor little buggers. A nasty fright for the pair of them.' He was moved by the plight of the children, but his desire to remain anonymous and avoid involvement overruled all other concerns. Engaging the gear lever, he made off at maximum speed. He was just too tired to deal with this and simply couldn't face the thought of stopping and becoming further involved. All he could focus on was getting far away from the scene as quickly as possible. No one was following as far as he could tell, but he kept up the speed, thankful that there were no other boaters to object to the excessive wash swirling against the banks. 'Those two fellows will be busy dealing with the kids and their mammy, never mind the burning boat – they've more than enough on their plate as it is.' He looked again at his canal guide and sighed as he counted up the locks that lay ahead. Despite his utter weariness, he decided to press on for a while and put more distance between himself and the incident.

The pall of black smoke spread above the scene, reminding him of the threatening thunder clouds that came rolling in over the mountains when he was a lad. His mother had told him that if he didn't behave, there was a bogeyman up there who was just waiting for an excuse to reach down his huge, hungry hand and snatch him away. The vivid nightmares induced by this terrifying threat had stayed with him for years.

His intention was to continue down to Brentford locks, cruise on the Thames towards Windsor, then see how far his fancy would take him. It was a pleasing prospect, and he hummed quietly as the boat rumbled on towards the first of the many locks. He felt weary but sublimely happy, stirring his coffee and nibbling on a chocolate biscuit as he contemplated the attended locks on the Thames.

What he couldn't know was that a young woman had captured his rescue of the children on her smartphone, and was at that moment playing the entire sequence back to her parents.

CHAPTER FIFTEEN

Of course, the footage appeared on social media, went viral almost at once, was picked up by the local paper and syndicated to the national press.

Questions such as 'Who is reluctant hero?' and 'Do you know mystery man?' appeared with pictures of Kevin lifting the children to safety, and a lurid article in one tabloid paper went so far as to suggest that he could well have been a paedophile who'd had second thoughts. Quite unaware of these developments, Kevin continued his leisurely journey towards Brentford lock.

A couple of days later, he enjoyed an early walk into Uxbridge for supplies, looking for a launderette and a decent toilet – such a wonderful morning, a pale mist rising from the canal as the sun burned through, promising another glorious day. He'd never felt happier and, after putting away his groceries, he phoned ahead to book a slot at Brentford Lock. He had just sat down to his breakfast when he felt the gentle sway as someone stepped on board. A shadow darkened his table and he looked up to see the jowled features of Brian Fitzgerald framed in the open doorway.

'Good morning, Oliver. Isn't this nice? We thought the newshounds would be beating a path to your door, still be all over you. Perhaps they've been and gone, eh?'

'How did you find me?' asked Kevin, determined to appear unfazed by the huge shock.

'Do you not read your paper, Oliver?' Fitzgerald nodded at

the newspaper lying on the settee where Kevin had tossed it.

'I don't buy one every day. And I like to have my breakfast first.'

'Here, try yesterday's.' Fitzgerald threw a tabloid paper down onto the table. 'Go on. Open it.'

Kevin turned the paper over and was astounded to see the picture of himself lifting the children from the water.

'That's you, is it not?' said Fitzgerald. That's how we found you and your *Happy Bloody Wanderer*. Read on and you'll see that the little lad told his mammy you're a nice man. He also told her you sounded Irish. But, on top of that, and here's the clincher, Oliver, he told her you were missing a finger. There you are, Mr Incognito, all over the news, a celebrity overnight, everybody's dream, eh? Wasn't it lucky for those kids that you came along when you did, eh, Oliver? We might never have found you, you crafty bugger. Never saw you as the jolly sailor. Well, your little deception is banjaxed now all right.'

'Who's we?'

'Tom Kelly's here and he's just as delighted to see you as I am.'

Kevin relaxed a little. He had no fear of Kelly, but Fitzgerald's presence was cause for concern.

'You might want to finish your bacon, Oliver,' said Fitzgerald. 'What is it they say? The condemned man ate a hearty breakfast.' He sniggered unpleasantly. 'I do like your little home,' he said, stooping to get a look beyond the dining area. 'Snug as a bug, eh?'

Kevin's thoughts went back to the previous day when a fellow boater, chatting while waiting in line at one of the many locks en route, said, 'Busy day yesterday, then?'

It had seemed such an odd remark, delivered with a knowing

look and now he realised its significance. Of course, the man was referring to the rescue of the children and not the physical demands of all those locks. Another had pointed at him, winked broadly, then joined with his wife in a round of applause as they cruised by in the opposite direction. It all made sense now. If only he'd bought a paper yesterday or put on the television, he would have been alerted by the news coverage – ready, not taken by surprise like this. What to do?

Fitzgerald was speaking again. 'I'm going to move back a bit so you can come up and join us, Oliver. Nice and slow, now – and keep your hands where I can see them.'

Kevin got to his feet, approached the short flight of steps and ascended. Stepping out onto the deck, he saw the gun in Fitzgerald's hand and the swarthy Tom Kelly just behind, also holding a weapon. Fitzgerald beckoned with his free hand, saying, 'Give me your gun, Oliver, butt first. Slowly now. Tom, eyes on the path if anyone comes along.'

Kevin reached into his smock pocket for the revolver and handed it over.

'Very nice,' said Fitzgerald, admiring the weapon. 'Short-barrelled Colt revolver. You always used an automatic, Oliver. It was your automatic that killed young Eugene, was it not?'

'That was accidental. It was in my hand, but I didn't pull the trigger. O'Brian's dog leapt at me, I lost my balance and the gun struck against a vice and went off.'

'Why run then, Oliver?'

'Why do you think?'

'The woman survived, you know.'

'Yeah, I read about it.'

'The woman survived; the bloody dog survived. You made a real bollix of a straightforward operation.'

'I was ordered to kill O'Brian, which I did. It wasn't me who shot the dog and the woman is alive because my bloody gun jammed.'

'Who shot the feckin' dog then?'

'Eugene.'

'Ah, so it was all down to Eugene, then? 'Course he can't deny it, can he, Oliver? Young Eugene can carry the can, eh? Old Oliver's in the clear – not his fault at all, eh? I don't think so, and neither will his Uncle Joe.'

'Now you see why I took off?'

'My orders are to locate your whereabouts and tell Uncle Joe where to find you, so he can settle with you and avenge the murder of his nephew in person. But I've been thinking. See, if your worthless carcass is found with this Colt in your hand – I'm talking suicide, Oliver – then he won't have to trouble himself. I'm going to disobey orders. I'm going to shoot you myself with your own weapon, Oliver, and put it into your dead hand. Isn't that a grand little scheme? No one will know what really happened except the two of us, eh? Just you and me, Oliver. But you won't count, of course.'

'What about him?' Kevin nodded towards Kelly.

'What about him?'

'He'll know.'

'Are you looking to finagle yourself some kind of advantage here, Oliver?' Trying to drive a wedge between me and my old pal Kelly? He'll never let on. He hates you nearly as much as I do. Anyhow, here's what we're going to do. You're going to drive your boat along this lovely river 'til I see a place suitable for my little project. Somewhere with lots of trees. So, let's get started. Oh, and if you try to tip the wink to anyone along the way, I'll have to shoot them too. You never know; afterwards, I might just take a holiday in your little boat. Yes, that would be nice, especially this lovely weather.'

'You'd never get your fat arse in the shower,' said Kevin.

Kelly put a hand over his mouth, trying to smother his amusement.

Fitzgerald just stood smirking, pointing the gun.

'Have your little jokes whilst you can, Oliver. It won't be long now.'

CHAPTER SIXTEEN

'I have to do a few checks first,' said Kevin.

'What are you talking about, checks?'

'Engine, oil and water, clear the propeller.'

'Are you trying to kid me, Oliver? Have you got one of your sly tricks up your sleeve?'

'Not at all. It's daily routine that's all, and you're holding all the aces,' he answered, shrugging, palms widespread.

'What exactly is it you have to do?'

'Undo this housing behind you for the propeller,' said Kevin, pointing to the inspection box. 'And lift this deck panel for the engine.'

'Feck you and your daily routine. Just untie her and get going. I'm looking forward to a ride on your dinky little barge, Oliver. Now, no more playing for time, eh.'

Untying the mooring ropes, Kevin stooped to pull up a stake.

'You can leave those,' said Fitzgerald, waving him back on board. 'You won't be needing them. You can tie up to a tree or something when we park.'

Kevin engaged the propeller and, as they drew away into the channel, he was assessing his chances. A mooring stake might have been handy in a fight, but how to get close enough? He was in no doubt of the sadistic Fitzgerald's intentions, and his position looked hopeless as things stood. *If he wants it to look like suicide, he'll have to come in close*, he pondered. *That might be the only chance I get, but it's cutting it very fine. Hope I can get at him sooner.*

He could only wait and be ready. *Tricky with two of them*, he mused, *but we'll see.*

They cruised on, the surface of the canal green with the bloom of duckweed flourishing after days of unbroken sunshine, Kevin keeping his speed down as they passed several moored boats where families and friends were enjoying late breakfasts or brunch or simply chilling out with a drink, contemplating another day of active cruising.

Fitzgerald looked most odd standing there in his dark suit and tie but seemed oblivious to the curious stares of passing boaters. He kept his gun down by his side, out of sight but ready and his eyes never left Kevin.

'Lock coming up,' said Kevin, pointing ahead.

'Where? What do you mean?' answered Fitzgerald, looking round, flustered.

'Look. Through the bridge. See the gates. Number 89.'

Fitzgerald, momentarily at a loss, looked ahead but regained his composure as they slid smoothly under the bridge and he saw the wooded area on the right where the canal widened into a basin.

'Pull over there,' he shouted, pointing. 'Under the trees.'

'We can't moor here. It's too near the lock,' Kevin countered.

'Just bloody do it, man. Get over there and tie her up. Tom, get up here and deal with any problems while we're gone. Anyone gets awkward, say I'll only be a few minutes.'

As he looped the rope round a low branch, Kevin felt a surge of hope at this unexpected halving of the odds. *Not very bright, Brian*, he thought. Tom, not known for thinking on his feet, standing there in his suit without a bloody clue. Kevin smiled at the thought then took a deep breath. *First things first*, he thought.

'Pull her back a bit,' ordered Fitzgerald. 'There's a bit of a path.'

Kevin slipped his knot, drew the boat backwards until Fitzgerald cried, 'Hold it, hold it there. That's it.'

He made fast.

'You first,' said Fitzgerald, gesturing with his free hand. Looking round, Kevin stepped off, down onto the narrow path leading into the woodland. They hadn't attracted any attention. *That could change when boats start arriving in earnest*, he thought.

'Off you go then, Oliver,' said Fitzgerald, giving him a shove in the back. 'None of your sneaky little tricks now. I'll tell you when to stop.'

Kevin trod lightly on the soft ground, making his way into the relative darkness beneath the dense canopy. Arriving at a small clearing, he stopped.

'Keep walking, you sly bastard,' said Fitzgerald. 'I'll tell you when to stop.'

'I was hoping you'd have a change of heart, Brian. We both know how Uncle Joe will react if he finds out you disobeyed his order,' Kevin said, over his shoulder.

'And how will he do that, you feckin' eejit?'

'I don't see Tom keeping his mouth shut if Joe starts quizzing him, do you? Especially if he has drink taken. Joe's no fool.'

'Shut your damn mouth and keep walking. Tom'll do as I say.' Kevin didn't move.

'I said keep walking, arsehole.' Kevin stood his ground, straining to hear the soft shuffling of leaves that would signal his abductor's approach.

'Get going,' said Fitzgerald, keeping his distance.

Kevin didn't move. Then he heard it, the soft sounds as cautious footsteps disturbed the dead leaves underfoot. Even so, he was unprepared for the violent blow that knocked him flat on his face, gasping to draw breath.

'Get up. Get up now, or I'll drill you where you lie, you tricky bastard,' shouted Fitzgerald, voice shrill, betraying his anxiety.

Kevin lay still, aware of the soft whispering of the leaves above where the faint breeze disturbed the treetops and carried the metallic *clink-clink, clink-clink* of ratchets as boaters worked the lock gates.

'Canal music,' he murmured, smiling to himself.

At last with a groan, he pushed up onto all fours, then onto one knee where he remained, breathing deeply, shaking his head.

'You die now,' cried Fitzgerald, his voice cracking with tension. He raised his gun and stepped forward.

'Time to piss yourself, Oliver bloody Flynn.'

Kevin whirled suddenly. The burst of gunfire and sudden whirring wings of fleeing birds shattered the peace of the wood. Kevin was marginally faster, though he flinched at the whizz of Fitzgerald's bullet, so close to his face, as he watched the big man collapsing, a confused expression on his florid face – killed instantly by the two small-bore rounds that drilled his forehead.

Total silence.

As his hearing came back, Kevin held out his hands, dismayed to see the tremor, as reaction to his ordeal began to take effect.

He looked at the body dispassionately, noting the head wounds. 'Two out of five,' he murmured. 'Not my best but good enough on the day.'

He put the small pistol to his lips and slid it back into his ankle holster.

'Christ, that was close,' he muttered. 'I'm too old for this.'

He remained on one knee, soothed by the soughing of the leaves, as he brought his breathing under control and collected his thoughts, caught in the accusative glare of Fitzgerald's dead eyes. The body lay among last year's leaf litter, Kevin's gun in its hand.

'I'll have that anyhow,' he murmured, getting to his feet and stooping to recover the weapon. Kneeling to check there was no pulse, he replaced the round in the revolver, pocketing the spent cartridge, then slipped behind a broad tree at the sound of approaching footsteps.

'Here comes your Kelly in a hurry,' he muttered.

Sure enough, Kelly's dark, bulky shape appeared out of the shady background as he came running along the path. 'Are you there, Brian?' he called breathlessly. 'Holy Mother of God!' he cried, pulling up as he saw the body. 'What the hell?-' He was silenced by the sight of Kevin stepping from his hiding place.

'Ah no,' he pleaded, raising his hands and staring at the gun in Kevin's hand.

'Throw the gun down there,' ordered Kevin, pointing.

Kelly tossed his pistol down, putting his hands in the air as Kevin patted him down. Satisfied, Kevin retrieved Kelly's gun and stood back.

'Pull up the legs of your trousers, Tom,' he ordered. 'You might just have a little gun down there.'

Kelly did as he was told and stood meekly, comical with his fat, white legs on show, while Kevin walked round to face him.

'Now,' he gestured toward the body, 'take out his gun and empty his pockets, then throw it all over here. Then, you're to drag your fat friend off the path and hide him back there somewhere. Then I'll decide what to do with you.'

'He was never my friend, Oliver,' said Tom. 'I had to partner him. Orders, you know, like you and Eugene.'

Kevin pocketed Fitzgerald's pistol and property, watching thoughtfully as the perspiring Kelly heaved the corpse in among the trees. It was the work of a few minutes to drag the body well back from view and roll it into a hollow. Once finished, Kelly steeled himself for the worst.

'Listen up now, Tom. You heard the shooting, I guess?'

'I did. It wasn't that loud back there, there's a lot going on. I heard it, but then I was listening for it. 'Course, I thought there would be just the one. Anyway, nobody seemed to take any notice.'

'Why' asked Kevin, 'did he go through this pantomime?' indicating the surrounding woodland. 'He had me cold there over my breakfast. He could have done away with me on the boat, shut the doors and left. Job done.'

'I guess he liked a bit of a drama, Oliver. Anyhow, he was a bloody sadist, you know. Bastard enjoyed it. Well, he sure came unstuck at last.'

'I'm going back to the boat. Did you have any bother there?'

'No. They were all busy manoeuvring their boats. It was very interesting actually; I was quite engrossed. They just got on with it, took no notice of me or your boat.'

'You stay out of sight 'til I'm gone. Then get yourself off home. Don't hang about. The body will be found soon enough and we need to be long gone from here. When it hits the news, people will remember the odd goings on and you two guys in your dark suits, like a couple of mafia hitmen. When you get back, I want you to tell Eugene's Uncle Joe my side of what happened with Conor O'Brian. Will you do that?'

'I will. I'll tell it the way you told us. I'll tell him it was an accident.'

'Good. Let's hope he believes you.'

'Well, I do, Oliver. I couldn't see you killing that lad the way they said. You know all is not well with Joe.'

'What do you mean?'

'He's not the man he used to be. He's going the way of his da.'"

'I'm sorry, Tom. You're losing me.'

'His father suffered with the dementia, Oliver, and it looks as though Joe's going the same way. He's about the same age as his father was when it became obvious he was unwell. Joe's showing the same sort of symptoms, forgetting stuff and then being very aggressive... it's always someone else's fault, you know. I think he knew in his heart that young Eugene was the wrong man for the job and I'm not the only one thinks that way, but having decided on him, he was never going to back down. He has big mood swings these days and you never know where you are with him. Something has to be done soon. It looks as though he'll be stood down – I wouldn't want to be there when that happens. If you can keep your head down 'til it's sorted, you might well be exonerated.'

'Thanks for that, Tom, but I wonder will the family forgive and forget? By the way, Oliver's gone for the time being, Tom. Call me Kevin, eh.'

'Kevin? Sure, if that's what you want. I'll try to remember.'

Kevin patted Kelly's shoulder, said, 'Safe journey, Tom,' and walked away along the path, towards the sunshine and the half-bottle of brandy in his sideboard.

CHAPTER SEVENTEEN

The *Happy Wanderer's* proximity to the lock made things rather tricky. She was so awkwardly placed that Kevin was going to find it hard to line her up and enter the lock. Boats were still passing through, though fewer in number than earlier, so while he waited for a suitable gap in the traffic, he sipped brandy, reflecting on his close call. True, he had come out on top because he always carried a second gun. But luck had been on his side too. They had fired almost together and he'd scored a hit, Fitzgerald a miss – but very close.

He'd been caught out because he'd become complacent, his guard down. True, he hadn't foreseen the media interest in his rescue of the children, but had he only stuck with his habit of keeping abreast of the news, he would have been forewarned, ready for trouble. If only he'd left the bloody beard alone, they probably wouldn't have recognized him in the first place. He felt somewhat warmed by the brandy but still a bit weak at the knees. *Shock won't be hurried*, he thought.

After starting up and unhitching the rope, he waited for a lull in the traffic then began to inch slowly towards the lock. Being so close and approaching at an acute angle, it was a matter of getting out to the middle of the pond, and rotating the boat on its axis until she was facing the open gates. A boat appeared under the bridge; the helmsman waved him ahead and backed up to give him room, engine racing loudly. Kevin kept his motor at idling speed, held the tiller hard over, watching as the bow swung round slowly until he was perfectly aligned. He increased his revs a tad, centred the tiller and glided into the lock. The second boat slid in alongside.

'Ah,' smiled the helmsman, 'I've been reading about you – rescued those children, very commendable.'

'Thanks,' said Kevin. 'For giving me room, that is.'

'Don't thank me. I was playing safe. I thought, if he makes a pig's ear of this, I'll stay out of his way 'til he's finished crashing and banging around. But there, you slotted her in a treat. Well done. Now, how about a drink while we're waiting? You can tell me all about it.'

'There's nothing much to tell,' said Kevin. 'They were in trouble so I pulled them out. Anybody would have done it.'

The man disappeared below, returning quickly with a bottle and two glasses. 'I don't usually share this one,' he said, pointing at the label. 'So you can count yourself privileged.'

'Actually, I've just had a large brandy.'

'Good as this?'

'Well, no, that looks a bit special.'

'Yes, it is. Courvoisier Reserve. Well over a hundred years old. Let me show my appreciation for your timely rescue of those kids. We'll drink to the family that's been spared a whole lot of grief because of your action.'

'Well, thanks, since you put it like that. I will, just a small one.'

'Good man. Here we go then,' he said, pouring the drinks carefully. 'Now, I think you're being much too modest,' he said, sipping appreciatively. 'People are awarded medals for what you did, you know. What do you think?' he asked, lifting his glass towards Kevin.

'It's wonderful,' replied Kevin, as the spirit warmed through his body. I've never tasted anything like it. It would revive a dead man, I think.'

The man threw back his head, laughing. 'Well, that's one recommendation I haven't heard before. That's a very nice craft you have there by the way, he said. Any chance of a look inside?'

'Sure thing. Come on over.'

Kevin followed the man down into his saloon, hand on the revolver's grip – ever suspicious.

'Now this is what I call high-end living,' said his visitor, gazing round with approval. 'Just look at this gorgeous panelling. Is it ash?'

'That's right. Previous owner spared no expense – went overboard as they say.'

'Not literally, I hope.'

'No, but he didn't live long enough to enjoy it. Would you like to see the rest?' They moved towards the bedroom via the shower cubicle and toilet, the visitor making complimentary remarks as they went.

'You certainly keep it all neat and tidy,' he said.

'Easy enough on my own. No one else to make a mess.'

'A place for everything and everything in its place, eh.'

'Something like that. Army training.'

'Would you consider selling her?'

'Not a chance. I'll be hanging on to her for a while yet.'

'Look, here's my card. If you change your mind I'd like first refusal.' They climbed out onto the deck.

'OK. Thanks,' said Kevin. 'You never know. I might feel differently come the end of summer – no promises, mind.'

'That was an odd place to moor up, wasn't it? Damned awkward to get away.' Kevin grinned sheepishly and sipped his drink.

'I was taken short actually – last night's curry. I decided a dump in the woods was preferable to stinking out the boat and I try to keep pumpouts to a minimum anyway — gets expensive.'

'On your own then, like me.'

'Yes. I prefer my own company. No one to talk back.'

'My wife's coming back on board at Brentford – been to see her elderly mother. I'll be glad when she's back – worn out locking by myself. I retired this year so we thought we'd spend the whole summer boating. Away from it all, you know – life in the slow lane if you like. The only paper I've bought recently was the one with you in it. Anyway, it's all been great so far. You don't look old enough to be retired.'

'Medical discharge,' said Kevin. 'I see you're a security consultant,' he said, looking again at the card.

'That's right. Can't spend all my time messing about on the boat. It supplements my pension – pays for winter mooring, servicing and so on.'

'What did you do before?'

'I was on the force. Kent County Constabulary, twenty-five years. What happened to your finger?'

'Legacy from my army days – shrapnel. Gulf War, the first one. This is why they let me go,' said Kevin, holding up his damaged hand.

'Whoops. Boats coming up. Time to get the gates open and get out of here,' the ex-policeman interrupted suddenly. 'Nice talking to you. Remember me if you do decide to sell her, you've got my number. I'll come up with a good offer.'

He took Kevin's glass, shouted his thanks to the arriving crew as they ran to swing open the gates, and motored out of the lock. Kevin, following on, cursed the fact that the man was ex-police. That bugger is going to remember every detail about me when the body turns up. Once a policeman, always a policeman – him and his bloody questions.

Well, he thought, *so much for keeping my head down. I was doing so well there for a while, but this changes everything. If only that boat hadn't caught fire, I'd still be going my own sweet way, Mr Nobody. My cover's blown as they say, blown to feckin' pieces. What to do now?*

CHAPTER EIGHTEEN

He cruised slowly, allowing the ex-policeman to get well ahead and soon enough, he was out of sight. *He's in a hurry to meet up with his missus,* he thought, *and that's fine by me. I've no wish to see him again.* The inopportune arrival of the retired policeman was a disastrous development. *As soon as Fitzgerald's body is found, which could be anytime soon, that man's testimony will be the end of me,* he thought. The only way out of this new difficulty he could see, was to take the body out of the equation. *And the only way to do that is to recover it,* he thought. *Recover it and find a more permanent hiding place – perhaps sink it in deep water, suitably weighted down. If there's no body to find, then I'm in the clear – nothing there to remind the copper of our friendly drink. I've still got a spare passport and bank account, but I've neither the time nor enough money to organise another disappearance.*

The more he thought about it, the more obvious it became that moving the body was his only feasible option. On reflection, it became clear that once the body was placed in a different location, its discovery wouldn't matter because there would be no reason to connect it with him. No press people had tried to contact him about the rescue, for whatever reason, and it was already old news, largely forgotten and unlikely to come back and bite him now. If there was follow-up, he'd just have to deal with it. Of course, after Tom Kelly tells his story, events in Belfast might go either way. But from what Tom had told him about developments over there, he felt there was a good chance he might be cleared of blame.

Anyway, whatever happens there, my immediate priority is to shift that bloody body. If that goes to plan, then I might be able to get back to being Mr Nobody, he thought.

And so, having made up his mind, he turned the boat at Cowley Peachey Junction and was soon on his way back. About twenty minutes later, he passed through the lock, cruised for about a mile, turned at a boatyard where he was able to buy a pair of mooring stakes, and made his way slowly back, ever watchful for signs of activity near the body. He tied up in the same place as before and waited...

All seemed quiet. Canal traffic had thinned out with the approach of evening, and he'd seen no sign of any disturbance when coming through the lock. As far as he could tell, the body still lay where Tom had left it – and no one the wiser. He would carry out a recce before it got dark, but the recovery would take place in the small hours, when he hoped the scene would be deserted.

The body lay a few yards from the path in a shallow depression, partially concealed by a large holly bush. Kevin studied the easiest route to drag it to the path and back to the boat.

'God Almighty,' he muttered. 'Will you look at the size of the bastard. I've got a job on my hands all right – like moving a bloody dead hippo. Old Tom is a strong bugger, but it's me that has to get it out of there.'

He made his way back to the boat to prepare, memorising any obstacles that would be tricky in the dark. Once on board, he cut lengths of cord and fashioned a harness affair of rope, which he would attach to one end of his gangplank. He intended to truss the limbs with cord, roll the body onto the plank, lash it in position and, using the harness, haul it back travois style. *Not ideal*, he thought, *but it's the best I can do. And that's after I kill myself getting it back up to the path.* Going forward, he opened the locker, where several items were stored, including a waterproof awning which he carried through to the rear deck, lifted onto the roof and partially unrolled. Then he placed his bedside unit, microwave oven and occasional table up there as well. His idea was to place the body on the roof, arrange the items of furniture around it to break up the outline and cover it with the awning so that it looked like a few pieces of furniture. *If anyone asks, I can say I'm delivering them for a friend*, he thought, as he covered the items. When his preparations were complete, he made a pot of coffee and settled down to wait for darkness.

He woke at 0220 and immediately set about his task. Out on deck, clad all in black and with a liberal application of mosquito repellent, he waited while his eyes became accustomed to the faint light of the crescent moon, then gathered his equipment in a supermarket bag, picked up the plank and moved quietly onto the path. At first the moonlight lit his way but, as he moved in among the trees, he had to pick his way in darkness. He'd measured the distances in paces and was well practised at moving at night.

'Funny how it all stays with you,' he said to himself, thinking back to his commando training. 'Like riding a bike, as they say.'

As he feared, dragging Fitzgerald's inert body back to the path was really heavy going. *How the hell did old Tom do it?* he thought, grunting and cursing as he strained to move the dead weight. At long last, after almost giving it up as a bad job, he somehow found the strength to move it the last few feet and lash it to the plank, ready to haul it back to the boat. He paused to recover his breath, listening all the time for danger. He'd made a lot of noise and was worried he might have attracted unwelcome attention. The night remained quiet, apart from an occasional rustling as some small creature went about its nocturnal business. He soon found that the travois idea had its problems, the main failing being a tendency to turn upside down, but he managed this by grasping the rope and walking backwards, dragging it a couple of yards at a time and resting in between.

At last, drenched in sweat and feeling totally worn out, he dragged his burden up onto the boat deck. It almost drained the last of his failing strength, but at last the body was up on the roof, wrapped in plastic, suitably disguised and relatively secure for the time being. He locked the doors and sat, chest heaving from his exertions, arms and legs turned to rubber and conscious of a tightness in his upper chest. It was 0330. Overcome by fatigue, he slept.

CHAPTER NINETEEN

At 0530 he woke with a start, feeling stiff and sore from the strain of his labours and itchy from several mosquito bites. The pain in his chest had gone. *Must have been a touch of indigestion*, he thought. There was no one about when he looked out, so he locked up and retraced his steps through the wood, making sure he hadn't dropped anything incriminating and disguising the worst of the gouges in the path. Just as he was going back on board, a woman appeared with a pair of frisky golden retrievers. As soon as she slipped their leads, they put their noses to the ground, circled and then rushed away, barking excitedly along the path and into the trees.

'Wow, they've found something exciting,' she cried, smiling at Kevin. He smiled back with an amiable nod, deciding not to betray his Irish brogue.

'Bloody hell,' he said to himself. 'Thank God I got him out of there in the night. Another close shave — got to get moving before the niff leads her bloody dogs back here. It's too early to get going yet, but I can move to the other side, ready for the lock.'

Fortunately, there was no sign now of the dogs or their owner. *There must be another way out*, he thought with relief. *Thank heaven for that.*

The day remained fine, growing warmer as he cruised away from Cowley Lock. Kevin was relieved to see no sign of the retired policeman's boat among those still at their moorings. *I reckon he's long gone*, he thought. *If I did come across him again, he'd surely smell a rat, literally. Now, where to dump this body?*

He considered exploring the Slough Arm in the hopes of finding a suitable place to offload his gruesome cargo, but he noticed another smaller arm on his map which promised to be less busy. This lay beyond Cowley Peachey Junction and was simply marked, "Ancient Waterway, channel navigable eight hundred metres to basin." *That might be what I'm looking for*, he thought. *Worth a look, anyway.*

A recently erected sign said "Eight hundred metres to basin". Kevin nosed the boat slowly into the opening, then took a sounding with his boathook. It showed a depth of about four feet.

'Seems OK,' he murmured. 'It's wide enough, anyway. Let's take a little trundle.'

Moving cautiously along the channel, he dipped the boathook several times and found the depth to be constant. This was better than he'd hoped for and seemed promising as a resting place for Fitzgerald's remains.

It was nothing like the well-tended canals to which he'd become accustomed. The banks were not defined by supports of any kind, clumps of reeds intruded into the channel, making it narrow in places, and he saw several holes. *That'd be the water voles*, he thought. Right on cue, there came a series of splashes and he spotted the vee-shaped wakes where a number of rodents were swimming hurriedly towards the safety of their burrows. In the space of a few minutes he saw three herons, the last of which descended through gaps in the canopy with impressive, acrobatic skill, then stood like a sentry, ready to fish.

He grew anxious as he progressed, although his soundings showed plenty of water. He had to keep an eye out for the many low branches which threatened to sweep away his rooftop cargo and he felt depressed by the air of neglect and abandonment. There was a sudden swash of water and he turned just too late. The water was still swirling where something large had plunged in. *Could it be an otter*, he wondered, *or maybe a big old bream?*

'Well, it's all back to nature all right, but it must be OK,' he told himself. 'They wouldn't tell you it's navigable if you couldn't turn to come out again, would they?'

Nevertheless, he was highly relieved when at last the basin came into view. The depth by this time had increased to about seven feet and the basin was larger than he'd imagined, with a solid-looking landing stage on the far side.

'Plenty of room then,' he said with relief. 'Maybe it's an old gravel pit. Now, let's have a look round.' He let the boat drift gently towards the middle of the basin, where he tried to take a sounding, but found that his boat hook was not long enough to touch bottom. 'Perfect,' he muttered as he cut the engine. 'Let's see,' he mused, looking round. 'If I wait for dark, I can roll him over the side here. He'll never be found in a million years. And even if he is, I'll be long gone. With the bullet wounds and his hands tied, the police might take him for a victim of a gangland killing – something local, drugs war or some such.' He looked across to the landing stage and decided to moor and have a look round.

The path leading from the jetty to the woodland was edged with boards and had been spread with crushed stone which looked recently laid.

'Someone keeps this place in good order,' he muttered. 'Let's have a look. Maybe a body could have been brought in this way. No boats involved.'

A short walk brought him to a car park where a lectern placed at the beginning of the pathway explained that this was a nature reserve and displayed pictures of the birds and small mammals one might encounter. It was headed, "Please respect our wildlife", and there was a litter bin placed close by. The bin being almost empty and the plastic liner quite new, Kevin deduced it was probably emptied regularly. Three cars were parked at the far side of the park and he noticed two other well-maintained paths, made obvious by the chippings, leading away into the wood.

'God Almighty,' he muttered, as the thought struck him. 'There's probably twitchers everywhere watching me right now.'

However, on walking back he saw no sign of anyone and it remained as quiet as the grave. A kingfisher flipped away, a blink of vivid blue, as he made his way back to the basin; he glimpsed it several times from his window as he made himself an omelette and settled down to wait for darkness. Once it sat perfectly still for several minutes. 'Now if I still had old Alan's camera, that would make a great frontispiece for my journal,' he mused. 'Mind, I have plenty of good ones already.' He heard the sharp call of a coot and watched it swim around the edge of the basin, its white face jerking like a child's wind-up toy.

With the approach of dusk, a swell of birdsong filled the air with an evening chorus such as he hadn't heard since his childhood. His thoughts went back to his boyhood home and that night his older brothers had dared him to go outside during a storm and shout at the bogeyman to go away. Of course, once he was outside, they bolted the door. He remembered the overwhelming terror that gripped him as he pounded on the door to get back in, the thunder rolling and booming overhead and the heartless laughter of the two of them inside. By the time his mother realized what was going on, he was a snivelling wreck. She gave out to the pair of them and cuddled him, crooning softly until he calmed down, but all the time the two of them were pulling faces at him behind her back. He'd nursed his grudge for a long time until he'd grown strong enough to exact revenge. Then he'd used his fists, beaten them both badly, taunting them all the while, telling them the bogeyman told him to do it. The elder, Joseph, tried to say sorry, but young Oliver broke his nose and loosened several teeth anyway. Two days later, Matthew received similar treatment. He'd not spoken to either of them since – didn't even know where they were...

'It wasn't just the night of the storm,' he murmured. 'Those two always gave me a hard time.'

He waited for nightfall.

The birdsong gradually petered out and he sat in the silence of that enchanting place, looking at the moonlight on the water, somewhat overcome by the magic of it all. *This is bloody amazing*, he thought. *You'd never guess I'm in outer London, one of the greatest cities in the world. I could be miles from anywhere.*

Taking a position amongst the trees, he watched the car park and soon heard voices approaching. A group of middle-aged men carrying rucksacks and tripods appeared from the opposite side and, after a few minutes of laughter and chatting as they loaded their gear, two of the cars drove off into the gathering dusk. About ten minutes later, a younger man, similarly laden, came crunching along the gravel path and drove away in the third car. Kevin hurried back to the boat. Walking back over the small stones, he had an idea, returned with a bag for life and filled it with chippings.

'Time to get on with it,' he told himself, 'now that everyone's gone home. Sooner I'm out of here the better. If I can dump old Fitzgerald and get out of here without being seen, most of my troubles could be over.'

CHAPTER TWENTY

He moved the *Happy Wanderer* back to the centre of the basin and, after pausing in the moonlight for several minutes but hearing nothing to alarm him, Kevin pulled back the awning, gasping at the stench and turning his head away as he brushed the sluggish blow flies into the water. He moved the items of furniture away from the body. There had been more deterioration after lying in the heat of the day. He could see through the plastic that the facial features were sagging, losing definition, and the torso had become swollen – it looked even fatter than before. The foul smell caught in his throat, making him gag – bloated flies were crawling everywhere.

Donning gloves, he took the bag of gravel and tied it firmly to the body, hoping this was heavy enough to overcome the buoyancy of the swelling corpse, drag it to the bottom and keep it there.

'God. Will I ever be rid of this awful stink?' he muttered, turning his head away in disgust.

He was ready to tip it overboard. Should he lower it slowly or simply give it a quick shove and hope the splash would go unheard? Caution prevailed, however, so he looped his centre rope around the body and lowered it gently into the water. Drawing his rope in and coiling it, he watched as the package rolled slowly then bobbed gently on the moonlit surface, buoyed by the gases trapped within. Cursing and crying with frustration, he seized the boat hook, thrusting violently as he tried to penetrate the layers of plastic sheeting, but it was too tough and the package continued to bob gently on the disturbed water. Driven to desperate anger, Kevin dashed below and seized the largest of his kitchen knives to cut through the tough material. Then as he returned to the deck, knife in hand, he forced himself to calm down. 'Come on,' he muttered. 'Think. You can sort this out without the panic. Go on like this and you're going to finish up sticking the knife in yourself.'

He found that by lying down and reaching out with the knife, he was able to stab through the plastic and hack open a long slit, a task made more difficult by the movement of the body on the water. Eventually, he managed to cut two long openings but despite his strenuous efforts, the package remained afloat.

Sitting there staring wearily at it, he felt defeated and was prepared to give up, to simply leave and hope for the best. But deep down he knew this was not good enough, so he bound the knife securely to the boathook and stood, shaking with fatigue. Then, steeling himself to the even more distasteful task, he thrust down time and again, piercing the swollen corpse, releasing more putrid air, until it began to sink at last, silvery bubbles trailing from the many vents, leaving him gasping to recover his breath as the moon's broken reflection danced on the gently rippling surface. He felt a huge sense of relief to be rid of it at last. 'Let that be the feckin' end of you,' he muttered. 'Fat pig!'

The furniture was soon moved below, but he decided to leave the awning, hoping it would air and that the persistent, bloated flies that still clung to it would soon lose interest and disappear.

Then, engine ticking over, he edged away into the channel and crept slowly back towards the Grand Union. It seemed an age before the junction came into view and he stopped just short, deciding to re-join the canal at first light. Completely worn out, he sank to his knees, curled up on deck and slept.

He was woken by water splashing his face. Blinking and spluttering in a moment of panic, he saw pale, grey, impenetrable mist while all around he could hear the constant dripping of water running off the leaves, falling like rain. Looking at his watch he saw it was just after 0500 and, after stretching to ease his chilled and aching body, he went below and soon had the kettle boiling for coffee. Shivering in his damp clothes, he stood recalling his nocturnal labours, holding the steaming mug between his hands, sipping cautiously at the scalding coffee. He could not be certain, but felt it was a pretty safe bet that no one had seen him dispose of Fitzgerald's remains. There was a good chance they would lie undiscovered at the bottom of the basin for a time – hopefully, a long time. There was nothing to identify the body and he'd got rid of the gun, wallet and passport, together with the rest of the contents of Fitzgerald's pockets, keeping the substantial wad of cash for himself.

'Home and dry?' he wondered. 'Bloody cold and wet actually.'

Looking forward to a hot shower and change of clothes, he ran the engine to heat the water.

By 0600, his ablutions completed and wearing warm, dry clothes, he manoeuvred the boat quietly out of The Fensford Brook back onto the canal, ready to resume his journey. The mist remained thick as ever. The kids' summer holidays will be over in a few days, he mused, then if we're lucky there'll be a bit of an Indian summer and then what? Approach of autumn, chilly, damp mornings and evenings – decision time looming nearer, close enough now to worry him.

'Breakfast,' he said, pulling himself together and finding a spot to moor. In a short time, the saloon was filled with appetizing smells of sizzling bacon, hot toast and coffee. *If I get good news from home,* he thought, *I can carry on as I am. Maybe lay her up for the winter and rent somewhere. Or I might find a temporary mooring and live on board. I'd be OK with the central heating and the wood burner; really snug. What if it's bad news though?* Finishing the last mouthful of bacon and spreading marmalade on the last piece of toast, he resolved to find a public phone and ring Tom Kelly's home number and find out what he could.

'Maybe Tom's on the level,' he murmured, 'or was he just saying anything to save his skin? 'He'll tell them I shot Fitzgerald too. What kind of a yarn will he tell them? Well, I hope I can find out soon enough.'

Looking out of his window, drinking a third cup of coffee, he saw that the mist was dispersing, promising yet another gorgeous day. Somehow it failed to raise his spirits…

He was woken by the ringtone of his phone. The Canal and River Trust, calling to confirm his time slot at Brentford Lock.

CHAPTER TWENTY-ONE

The run down to Brentford was uneventful and provided Kevin with many points of interest. Descending through the impressive Hanwell Flight turned out to be straightforward enough and he cruised on slowly, taken with the wooded scenery and well-tended grassy banks, astonished by the fact he'd come down close to a hundred feet. Brunel's three bridges, the iron trough, the long brick wall enclosing Ealing Hospital grounds and other locations of historic interest, all described in his guide, kept him busy with his camera, capturing images for his journal.

One minute he was gliding through sylvan woodland, a world away from the city; the next he faced a succession of scenic surprises. The juxtaposition of eighteenth-century technology with modern steel and concrete bridges and high rise buildings amazed him. It had been much the same when he'd left Camden to go north, but still he found it awesome.

'It's like a timeline in three dimensions,' he mused. Gazing up as he passed under the huge road bridge carrying traffic at speeds unheard of in days gone by, he smiled. 'Layers of time. Something for everyone I suppose… bit of nostalgia for the likes of me and state of the art modernity for those who like it. We can't all be the same. I guess it was always so. This canal was state of the art in its heyday.' He thought again about his forbears toiling to carve out the channel so long ago.

'Picks and shovels, day in, day out in all weathers. God, it must have been relentless hard graft – dangerous too. Small wonder the navvies had a reputation for drinking. It's a bloody monument to Irish brawn and stout,' he smiled.

As he approached Lock 101 he was pleased to see the gates crack open to reveal boats inside preparing to come out. Slowing, he hung back as they streamed past, returning nods and waves as he studied the moored boats to determine if there was a queue. No one looked as if they were ready to move, however, so he glided on and into the lock.

'Looks like it's just you then,' said the keeper, passing Kevin's ropes around the bollards. 'No. Hang on. Let's move you over. There's another one close behind.' Kevin turned to see a narrow boat sliding in next to him – a much larger vessel, seventy feet or so with a collection of plants in decorated containers as well as several bicycles on the roof. A balding, rather stout man stood at the tiller, his plump wife next to him and a teenaged boy and older looking girl were sitting on the roof. These two jumped down nimbly, obviously well-versed in locking procedures, and looped their ropes around the bollards ready for the descent.

'Come far today?'

Kevin looked across to see the man addressing him.

'Cowley Peachey Junction,' he replied. 'But I'm in no hurry.'

'We've come down from Slough, going on up towards Oxford. Been on the Thames before?'

'Not the tidal stretch, but I've got all the necessary gear, long rope and anchor. I'm headed same as yourselves, up to Oxford and maybe on up to Letchlade. I was up there years ago.'

'On your own?'

'That's right – hard work sometimes, but people are usually pretty helpful. I've come a long way down the Grand Union in the last few days but I take my time – often have a rest – cup of coffee and admire the scenery. You can't whack it.'

'That's true. There's six of us altogether – two more inside – so we share the hard labour, or rather the youngsters do,' he added with a grin. He put his arm around his smiling wife. 'We're best employed in a supervisory role – keeping an eye on the serfs, making sure they do things properly, that sort of thing.' This last remark brought a burst of good-natured jeering from the pair handling the ropes. The keeper joined in with, 'Oh, I do like to see a happy ship.'

Then it was time to exit. Down the River Brent for a few hundred yards, then onto the Thames.

CHAPTER TWENTY-TWO

Having negotiated Richmond and Teddington locks without incident, Kevin continued up to Molesey where he made an overnight stop and was at last able to contact Tom Kelly at home. He listened to the ring tone, hoping he'd struck lucky this time and was most relieved when Tom came on the line.

'Tom Kelly.'

'It's me, Tom.'

'Oliver? You OK?'

'I told you it's Kevin now.'

'Ah, sorry. I forgot. You OK?'

'I'm fine. Do you have any news for me?'

'Not yet. Sure it's early days still. There's a lot going on right now. In the end, Joe was stood down without a murmur. I still find it hard to believe. They say he seemed relieved – seemed glad to go in the end. I think Liam convinced him he wouldn't be able to hide his symptoms for much longer. It took everyone by surprise anyway. So there's big changes going on here just now.'

'I'm wondering where that'll leave me?'

'See, Kevin, I know there's a lot riding on this for you, but right now it's not a priority at this end. What I can say is Liam questioned me and I'd say he's on your side even though the lad was his nephew. He thinks if you'd done what was said, you'd never have let me come home.'

'What do they say about your partner?'

'Well, no one was surprised he was disobeying orders. The

general feeling is he had become unreliable, bit of a loose cannon, you know, too big for his boots. Joe found him to be unsatisfactory too, sloppy was his word for him, not a man to trust at all. No one's said as much but it seems he's no great loss.'

'You told them how it happened?'

'I did.'

'So, they know how to find me?'

'Not at all. I told them what happened but not where. I said we took you onto Wimbledon Common but then you got the better of him and asked me to come home and put your side of things. I told them you'd be well away from there by now.'

'That's it?'

'That's right. Is the fat man where we saw him last?'

'No. He had to leave there. He's gone.'

'I'd say you're going to be OK, Kevin. Ring again in a couple of days. I hope I'll have more for you.'

'I will, Tom. Thanks for what you did. Thanks a million.'

'That's OK, Kevin. Ring me, yeah?'

'You can count on it. Thanks again.'

Kevin ended the call and sat staring at his phone. His initial optimism began to drain away as he re-ran the conversation in his mind. *If Tom's on the level, I can carry on as I am. But is he? Can he be trusted? Is the plan to lure me back and settle the score? Liam is family, after all – he could tell Tom anything just to get me back there. I can't know for sure. I just have to hope Tom's not been got at. If it went down the way he says, then he's gone out on a limb for me. Why would he do that? Is it because I let him home?*

He spent a troubled night trying to work out his next move, but eventually decided it was out of his hands – nothing he could do was going to change anything. But he would be prepared for unwelcome visitors this time. He would not be caught napping again.

The bright morning sunshine helped to dispel his dark mood and, after breakfast and the daily maintenance tasks on the boat, he gathered his ropes and continued upstream towards Sunbury. Showers were forecast for later in the day, but the morning stayed warm and sunny.

A couple of hours later, he locked at Penton Hook, found a mooring and walked along to the Crown for lunch. The effects of the meal and two large glasses of Merlot, together with having had a poor night's sleep, left him feeling dozy, so on returning to the boat he locked up and had a snooze. Waking refreshed, he cast off and cruised up to Boveney, where he moored for his second overnight stay on the river. His optimism was returning, nourished by the sheer pleasure of cruising on the Thames.

The promised showers arrived that night, drumming heavily on his roof but failing to disturb his slumbers.

CHAPTER TWENTY-THREE

All was not well with Kevin when he woke the following morning. He got up later than usual, his spirits at a low ebb and even his favourite breakfast, scrambled eggs and smoked salmon, failed to cheer him up. After a few mouthfuls, he scraped it into the waste bin. The weather, though grey to begin with, brightened, the cloud cover dispersing gradually, making way for a bright showery day. But he remained despondent. Breakfast over, everything tidied away, he sighed, went out and saw to the daily maintenance tasks. The awning, held in place by the gangplank and centre rope, was steaming in the sun, drying rapidly after the night-time downpour and, as far as he could tell, was now odour-free. *Must let that dry properly before I stow it away*, he thought.

By 11.30, he had reached Bray and gone through the lock, but it was a joyless journey. He could find none of his usual pleasure in simply cruising along taking in the scenery; it all required too much effort. It was beyond him. Consulting his guide, he decided to go through another couple of locks and then have a bit of a rest. *I'm out of sorts is all, knackered after all that heavy lifting*, he thought. *Forty winks could work wonders.*

As he continued towards Boulters Lock, he wondered about the reorganisation going on in the brigade and what the outcome might mean for him. Could he ever return or would they write him off as expendable – damaged goods? Such gloomy thoughts did nothing to boost his low morale.

'I'll need to buck up my ideas in a minute,' he muttered. 'There'll be quite an audience at Boulters according to the guide.'

***

'I vote we give Cookham a miss today and turn for home, my dears. There are lots more showers in the offing, judging by those dark clouds. We don't want a soaking.' Fiona's mother laughed. 'Mind you, it makes no difference to these water babies,' she continued, regarding the wet dogs fondly. 'They're in the river as much as they're out of it.'

'Yes, and shaking themselves all over us in between dips,' laughed her father. 'I do agree. But let's watch a couple more boats go through while we finish our coffee. There's still plenty in the thermos and I'm enjoying the sun. Even these three are enjoying a bit of a bask,' he said, indicating the panting dogs lying at their feet. 'What do you say, Fiona?'

'I'm happy to sit a little longer – make the most of the sunshine while it lasts,' she replied.

'There we are then,' said Father. 'The majority has it.'

He doled out the remaining coffee and the dogs became alert as Fiona passed round the Kit Kats.

'No chocolate for you guys.' She laughed, throwing them a handful of dog treats, amused by their frantic scrabbling and jostling. 'What a performance,' she laughed. 'Their nails are way too long. I'll fix up a vet's appointment on Monday.'

People began to drift away in twos and threes as the first plump raindrops dimpled the surface of the river. Fiona finished her coffee and stuffed the chocolate wrapper into her pocket, making ready to leave.

'What on earth's the matter with Bruno?' her mother called

suddenly.

The big dog stood, hackles raised, growling, staring downstream.

'Bruno,' called Fiona. Then more forcefully, 'Bruno! Come.'

The dog glanced her way briefly, but stayed put, one forepaw raised. His growling increased in intensity. Jack and Jill joined him, tails wagging as though this was some new game.

'He's watching that boat,' said her father, looking mystified. 'Come on. Let's put them on the lead and get out of here. This is turning into quite a heavy shower.'

Following her father's gaze, Fiona studied the approaching narrow boat, puzzled by Bruno's aggressive behaviour. She clipped the leash onto his collar and made to pull him away but he resisted, remained immovable, the deep, rumbling snarl now constant; ears flattened, front teeth bared. Suddenly, for the first time ever, she was afraid of him. The boat was heading into the lock when the man at the tiller gave them a wave and shouted, pointing up at the gathering clouds.

'Get your brollies up quick, ladies. Here it comes again.'

Bruno slipped his collar at the same moment Fiona heard the voice and saw the hand with the missing finger. Stunned as she recognized the assassin, she saw Bruno's prodigious leap onto the boat and watched him run along the cabin roof and hurl himself down onto the man. Too late, Kevin raised an arm to ward off the flying dog, but the force of the impact carried them both over the rail and into the water with a huge splash.

Kevin tried to scream as the powerful jaws closed on his throat – but he was submerged and struggling to prise himself free. He gave up when the lightning bolt exploded in his chest. His last thought as he wrapped his arms tightly round the dog was, *We'll go together then, you brute.*

As the *Happy Wanderer* motored into the lock, nosing the upper gates, Jack and Jill ran up and down barking furiously, plunged in and swam to where Bruno had gone under. The lock keeper jumped down onto the boat, stopped the engine and secured it. Fiona and her parents called the two springers repeatedly, but they continued swimming round and round frantically. They stared at the spot, willing Bruno to surface but all they could see were the anxious spaniels swimming – round and round – round and round. But no Bruno.

The hubbub of excited voices, growing louder as new arrivals demanded to know what was happening, impinged on Fiona's consciousness as she became aware of her mother's encircling arms. Hands clamped over her ears, blinking at the rain mixing with her tears, she watched numbly as her father caught Jill and continued calling desperately to Jack. Then she found herself confronted by an angry group of people as a large, belligerent man jabbed his finger into her shoulder shouting into her face, 'That poor bugger never had a chance! Your fucking dog has killed him. You know that?' Her mother interposed herself between them, forcing the aggressor to retreat several paces. Then her father was there, demanding order, fending off the hostile knot of onlookers while Jack and Jill, and half a dozen other dogs, were adding to the clamour, barking excitedly as two young men dived repeatedly, trying to locate the bodies.

Then a police patrol car arrived, and the two officers moved in, quickly imposed a semblance of order, and persuaded the two young men to come out of the water. Shortly after, they were reinforced by the arrival of a second car and the business of taking witness statements began.

Fiona, wrapped in her father's coat, had explained to her parents who the man on the boat was and how she'd recognized him just as Bruno got away from her.

'I know it sounds far-fetched,' she said, in response to their incredulity. 'Perhaps I've not explained it clearly, but I recognized that voice immediately and it's obvious Bruno knew who it was. Why else would he have attacked like that? He was never an aggressive dog. Come on. You know him as well as I do. Did,' she added, correcting herself, wiping away more tears.

Moments later her father reappeared with a female police constable in tow, saying, 'You need to hear this, Officer.'

CHAPTER TWENTY-FOUR

Fiona yawned and turned over to look at her bedside clock. It was 0600. She stretched luxuriously, revelling in the thought that this was her first Saturday off for several weeks. Her new job at a local estate agency was enjoyable, but it often entailed working at weekends so now she was contemplating a whole blissful weekend off. Her employer had quickly recognized her abilities, Fiona having worked previously in an estate agency, and she'd soon found herself negotiating the sales and purchases of expensive, upmarket properties in her area. Thameside properties were going for enormous sums; it was a revelation to her that such ordinary-looking folk had so much money. She was beginning to enjoy life again. The nature of the job involved socialising, keeping busy and meeting clients and, although there was more paperwork than she cared for, it suited her perfectly. She was too busy to dwell on past events and her night-time terrors had almost ceased completely. Her doting parents, always supportive, encouraged her to get on with her life. She would never forget Conor and the good times in Ireland, but her grief was becoming bearable at last, thanks in large part to the efforts of her new counsellor, a softly spoken, patient Scotswoman with a delightful west coast accent.

Throwing back the duvet, she stood, padded across to the window and drew back the curtain. Rain was forecast for the evening, but the new day was heating rapidly as the morning sun beamed from a clear blue sky. She could see her father moving about in his greenhouse, no doubt watering his precious tomatoes, peppers, cucumbers and melons, even at this early hour. He used rainwater for preference but now the water butts stood empty after weeks without any significant rainfall. She'd never really understood his passion for growing his own vegetables. He would insist that homegrown produce tasted better than shop-bought, but she thought that even if it were so, the difference didn't warrant all the hard work and expense. Her mother claimed it stemmed from his rural upbringing and memories of post-war rationing.

The kitchen garden bore testament to her parents' devoted efforts, everything neat and tidy: regularly spaced, carefully measured rows of root crops stood like soldiers on parade; several kinds of beans – including her favourite, runner beans – the small orchard and the walk-in cage where soft fruits ripened, safe from the predatory birds, were all lovingly tended. The rest of their large garden was equally well kept: neatly edged lawns, shrubberies and rose beds with several tranquil corners in which to relax with a book and an occasional glass of wine. Homegrown therapy, as her mother called it. Her father, however, in acknowledgement of their advancing years, had at last engaged a part-time gardener to cope with the heavier work.

The fenced-off area with kennels provided the dogs with a space to call their own. Here, they buried their bones, dug them up again and fought each other. Bruno had been happy there and, apart from these occasional, short-lived spats, the three dogs had got along very well. Now she gazed at the block of granite bearing his name, standing between the two remaining kennels.

She and her father had dug his grave and laid him to rest on one of Conor's shirts she'd used as a nightdress. The raw blisters on her hands had healed quite quickly, but not the grief. She had wept endless tears for her loss, but gradually it became easier to bear, attenuated by the passing of so many busy days.

The discovery that the drowned man had been carrying firearms and ammunition had given credibility to her story and the subsequent, lengthy enquiries had eventually led to his identification as a wanted IRA killer. She'd thought she would hate him forever, but nowadays he hardly ever crossed her mind.

She let the curtain fall back. Having a Saturday off this late in the year with the weather looking set fair for most of the day, she decided it was time to take a long walk with the dogs, maybe up to Cookham Lock and back. *It might well be the last time without wellies*, she thought. *Once the rain does come, it could set in for ages.*

'Are you sure you want to do that, dear?' said her mother, frowning at her husband across the breakfast table.

'Yes, I think so,' Fiona replied. 'It's been an absolute age since we took that walk. You know how the dogs love the river.'

And so, the three of them, each shod sensibly and leading the scatty pair of spaniels, now showing traces of grey round their muzzles but still bounding with energy, set out to walk the five miles or so to Cookham Lock.